THE DEVIL YOU KNOW

"I might be better behaved if you brought me something to eat—you can satisfy at least one of my hungers."

With a swish of skirts, she strode to the door. There she paused. "When were you ever satisfied with anything, Paxten? I shall have your beefsteak sent up to you."

She slammed out of the room. He stared at the door a moment, then chuckled. The Alexandria he had once known would never have slammed a door. It seemed he was not the only one to have changed.

But had she stayed with him simply out of responsibility? Because of the memory of affection? No—he could not believe that. She had stood still in his hold, her face indifferent, but the pulse had quickened in her wrist. She still loved to lie to him.

He smiled again, but without any humor, for he had just begun. With her, he would prove himself an utter devil. But first he would have to earn her trust. And that meant starting to act like the gentleman he had never been.

LADY SCANDAL

Shannon Donnelly

ZEBRA BOOKS
KENSINGTON PUBLISHING CORP.
http://www.zebrabooks.com

ZEBRA BOOKS are published by

Kensington Publishing Corp.
850 Third Avenue
New York, NY 10022

All Kensington titles, imprints and distributed lines are available at special quantity discounts for bulk purchases for sales
promotion, premiums, fund-raising, educational or institutional
use.

Special book excerpts or customized printings can also be created to fit specific needs. For details, write or phone the office
of the Kensington Special Sales Manager: Kensington Publishing Corp., 850 Third Avenue, New York, NY 10022. Attn.
Special Sales Department. Phone: 1-800-221-2647.

Zebra and the Z logo Reg. U.S. Pat. & TM Off.

First Printing: July 2004
10 9 8 7 6 5 4 3 2 1

Printed in the United States of America

For Uncle Bert and Aunt Barb,
who taught me how to shoot a flintlock
and ride sidesaddle

One

She had not thought of him in ages, so why had his memory returned tonight? Alexandria frowned. Had it been Josephine's insistence on dredging up stories of when she had been young and ridiculously romantic? Or perhaps it had been watching Diana flirt with the young—and utterly ineligible—Monsieur Brenton? Marsett had been just so ineligible—and just so charming.

But she would not think of him again tonight. She had other worries to fret over.

Still, she stared out the carriage window at the endless darkness that lay beyond the shallow yellow glow of the lantern, at the glisten of raindrops on glass. And she thought of another night such as this, in another carriage, in what almost seemed another life.

Bad weather making old injuries ache.

He was an old injury. Old and one she had thought forgotten. But tonight, as the carriage rocked, she remembered too well that strong, angular face, the unruly brown hair, the smolder of dark brown eyes. And the hot betrayal that had glittered in those eyes the last time she had seen him.

She had almost given up everything for him. Almost. And the old anger flared, still rankling for his having forced her into the worst moment of her life. Why had he not been able to understand?

And why did you not come back? Why did you never keep that promise?

But why would he? He must hate her now. She knew that.

The regret trembled inside her again, not as strong as it once had, but still there, along with the anxiety. Had she made the right choice? What else could she have done? She had had Jules to consider. Bitterness tugged at her, a weight in her chest. She fought it back, willing it away, determined that it would drag no more futile tears.

But still she thought of him.

Where would he be tonight? At a gaming table? In another woman's arms. He had always loved excitement. Did he still? Was his hair as dark and lush, or had those silky strands thinned, or acquired touches of silver as now threaded her brown curls? Would he still have that broad chest and those muscles that rippled under her touch and that smooth skin, so warm and. . . .

"You are very quiet, Aunt."

Blinking and pulling in a breath, Alexandria turned away from the darkness outside the carriage. The lanterns spilled a faint glow into the luxurious gloom of the coach, outlining swaying curtains, the plush upholstery, and her niece's delicate profile.

They ought to have been back in Paris by now. It was only a few hours from the duke's Château d'Esclimont. But a horse had thrown a shoe, and then the rain had started, turning the road into mud that dragged at the carriage wheels.

Alexandria forced a smile, then she realized that Diana would not see it—all she could see of her niece was the glint of her golden curls and the white oval of her face. Years of practice at hiding her feelings, however, kept her voice utterly calm. "I am just longing for a hot cup of tea."

Such a lie. What she longed for had nothing to do with tea. She scowled at her weakness.

Diana's gloved hand, almost ethereally pale in white kid, reached out from the darkness of her traveling cloak to grip Alexandria's. "It cannot be much farther. Look, you can see the lights of Paris already."

Alexandria's face relaxed. How like her niece to be the one to try and reassure. She leaned across the leather-covered seat to glance out the window. Lights did glint through the gloom—the flambeaus of the great houses, lanterns for the scandalous Palais Royal and the Comédie Française; the entertainment of Paris did not stop for weather nor for much else, it seemed. Not even with war threatening again.

Alexandria squeezed her niece's hand and then she leaned back, the leather squeaking under her. Their plans had been to stay another month in Paris before returning to England, but the duke's cautions had changed everything.

"You should leave France," Josephine's husband had said, his English accented heavily and his tone grim. Josephine had wrinkled her nose as she made a noise that could sound elegant only when coming from a Frenchwoman. "Really, Guy—how rude to tell my friends to go."

He had frowned at her, a sober older gentleman, his thin face and thinning hair making him look more dour than usual. "Less rude than if they should be here when the battles start again. And they will. This peace cannot last—not with England refusing to leave Malta. Not with—"

He broke off, his mouth pulling down, as if he had had to stop himself from saying something unwise, such as to criticize the ambitious First Consul Bonaparte.

Josephine waved away his words, her plump hand fluttering and her jewels flashing. "War . . . war . . . you have been too long in the military, *mon trésor*. Everyone muttered the same in March, when Bonaparte accused Lord Whitworth of forcing us into breaking the peace. But nothing happened, now did it?"

"Whitworth has left France. Word came today. It cannot be good that the British ambassador leaves so sudden."

Josephine had frowned, but then she laughed and demanded that he not ruin her house party by troubling her English friends.

But he already had.

Alexandria knew to give his warning added weight. The Duke of Laval had survived the bloody Revolution, saved from his country's anti-aristocratic insanity by his military titles and success. With Bonaparte now ruling France, the duke no longer needed to call himself citizen—Bonaparte had done away with that and much else from the Revolution. And gossip held that Laval would soon be a marshal of France. If such a highly placed man thought hostilities would come again, Alexandria knew enough to listen.

Perhaps that was why the anxiety, the troubling regrets, had returned. She might have made mistakes with her own life, but she would not make them with her brother's only daughter.

Now wistful disappointment tinged Diana's voice as she asked, "Are you certain we cannot at least stay until after Madame Avill's ball? I am still due a gown from Celeste's for it, and . . . and. . . ."

"And there is a certain young man you hoped to see again at Madame Avill's?" Alexandria asked, unable to resist teasing.

"Oh, that is nothing serious. You know that, only—well, isn't Monsieur Brenton just the most ravishing gentleman you have ever met? And he does dance divinely, and I did promise him one dance at Madame Avill's."

He was not the most ravishing gentleman Alexandria had met—he seemed young, absurdly so. However, she knew the sound of youthful infatuation. She also knew the importance of allowing such sparks to burn out so that they left warm memories and not bitter laments.

But she could not ignore Laval's warnings.

Frowning, she tried to make the right choice. Would a few days matter? That would allow a more organized departure—and she could write to Frederick to let him know she would be bringing Diana to London, not to his Surrey estate, as they had arranged. But what if she judged wrong? So many others had already left France.

Well, she knew the lack of wisdom in making any decision by moonlight. "We can discuss it in the morning," she allowed.

Diana's hand clutched hers. "Oh, thank you, Aunt Ali."

"I said discuss—and I mean only that."

"Of course, Aunt."

Diana sounded dutiful. She also sounded confident of the outcome.

Leaning back in the coach, Alexandria shook her head. She indulged the girl. Too much, perhaps. But she had only ever had Jules—her independent, bookish son, now up at Oxford. And girls, she had learned from Diana, were ever so much more fun.

By the time they reached the cobbled streets of Paris, Alexandria's longing for tea had become genuine. So had her hunger for a hot meal and a seat that did not sway.

They entered the city through the north gate, skirting the village of Montmartre and its steep hill. The narrow cobbled streets had hardly been changed, Alexandria thought, by revolution or the centuries. Bonaparte talked of building wide new avenues, but parts of Paris, within its stone walls, echoed back to its ancient roots, with its winding lanes, barely wide enough for a cart, let alone a carriage. A decade ago, the French queen and king had been bundled into such carts and dragged by the mob to the guillotine. Had they been carried along this very road?

Alexandria shivered. She hoped not.

But blood no longer ran in the gutters. For all his faults of ambition, Bonaparte had at least brought order to France. And he had made peace with England just over a year ago, leaving the door open for so many to come again to Paris. It had been a delight to bring Diana, and such a relief to escape her own monotonous life.

They had taken a small house for their visit—with the jointure left to her, she could afford to indulge her whims these days. But even after two months in Paris, she recognized few landmarks. It was only when the coach stopped and the door opened and she glanced out that she knew they had arrived at 37 Rue Cambon. They were home.

The footman helped her from the carriage, and she glanced up at the house, a little surprised to see it dark and the front door standing ajar. Fenwick was not the sort to shirk his duties. So where was her butler? Why were there not lamps lit beside the steps? Why did no one hurry from the house with umbrellas and see to their luggage?

With a frown, Alexandria glanced around her.

The rain had lightened to a mist, slicking the streets and leaving the sky dark. The buildings seemed to huddle close, their stucco walls pale in the dim light and their roofs disappearing into darkness. Pulling the hood of her traveling cloak over her bonnet—a silly little velvet one she had bought just for the visit to the Château d'Esclimont—Alexandria hurried up the steps. Her traveling boots slapped against the puddles left by the rain. Pushing open the heavy door to the house, she stepped inside and stopped. Shock chilled her skin.

"What in heaven's—"

She broke off the words, the air tight in her chest. Irritation sharpened in her, then chilled into fear.

Flowers lay strewn across the floor as if emptied from the vases that had once held them. She glanced around the hall, looking for those vases and seeing only unsettling disorder. A chair lay on its side. The wire dangling from the picture rail told of a painting taken away.

A soft voice at her side pulled her attention from the disaster in the room. "Oh, my! What happened?"

Alexandria turned. She parted her lips to reply—only what did she say to her niece?

And then the sound of a woman's soft sobbing reached her, chilling her utterly.

He was lucky not to be dead. Pain, sharp and raw, burned in his side. He cursed in guttural French, and then in English, the hard Anglo-Saxon sounds far more satisfying. He kept the curses to a low mutter, however, wary of giving himself away.

Three hours earlier he had been in a warm bed with an equally warm armful of woman. A general's wife in need of consolation for a husband who neglected his duties to her. But then he had said the wrong thing.

Never call one woman by another woman's name.

He knew that law of dalliance. But he'd had another woman too much in his thoughts of late—*merde,* why had he ever listened to the gossip? Why had he stayed after hearing her name mentioned?

It was, of course, only curiosity. He had not thought her the sort to ever leave her cozy home. But she had apparently come to Paris, along with so many other English. And with a niece in tow. A beautiful girl, according to those who had met her. Golden hair, soft blue eyes, and oh-so-English alabaster skin. He had smiled and nodded at the descriptions, but his mind had filled with brown, softly curling hair that had once twined around his fingers. He had remembered gray eyes, and slanting, light-brown eyebrows that tipped up in the center when a smile lifted her wide mouth. And those slender curves and pert breasts that fit so well into his hand . . . rather too like Madame D'Aeth's.

Which was why he had used that once-forgotten name instead of Madame's.

Stiffening, she had glared at him.

And then she had started to scream.

He'd had time to grab his breeches and his coat. He left his cravat and fled. He had almost been over the garden wall when the ball from the musket caught him, scraping across skin and muscle and rib as it etched a groove in his side. He had felt nothing more than a sting at the time. But as he ran, half stumbling as he struggled into his clothes, the pain began to burn.

That's what he got for bedding the wife of a military man. Other households had servants, not guards with muskets. And now he had best move on before they backtracked to pick up his trail—thank God for the rain and the dark night.

Wincing, he eased his palm from his side. Sticky wetness clung to his shirt and his fingers. Still bleeding. Damn! He pressed his hand to his side and his back to the wall.

He had found temporary shelter in an alley off the Rue de Turenne, far too close to the D'Aeths' mansion. And uncomfortably near the Bastille. A sign that perhaps he ought to quit Paris—and perhaps even France. Bonaparte's generals carried far too much power, and no one would question the death— or imprisonment—of one such as him.

But where to next?

Eyes shut, Paxten leaned against the wall, soul weary, body aching. Where could he go? Back to Italy? To Venice perhaps, and the contessa with the lazy eyes and the jealous streak? That seemed unwise. To the Americas, or to India? He had not been either place yet, but that meant a long ocean voyage. An uncomfortable one, too, with his funds so low.

Boot heels on cobblestones clattered near to him. Voices rose and then receded, taking their anger with them. Pushing off the wall, he pulled in a breath, then winced at the searing pain. Shallow breaths only. He needed something to bind the wound, to stop the bleeding. And a decent cognac to dull the aches.

Could he make it back to his lodgings? It was not far to the Place des Vosges, where he had taken rooms—on a whim to stay near the square where knights once jousted to honor Anne of Austria's marriage to a French king. But if Madame had betrayed his identity to the guards as well as his presence in her boudoir, would it be safe?

With a grimace, Paxten staggered into the street, his legs unsteady and his head light. God, how much had he bled?

He tried to weigh his options. He had a few coins in his coat pockets—a good thing he had won tonight at the tables. Did he have enough to reach the border? Perhaps, but not in style. And there was the matter of transportation after that— and lodging. He would also need new clothes. He hated to leave his current ones—he had only recently had most of them made— but he had done that before. His mouth twisted.

What, after all, did a man such as him own that could be of value? No, he had nothing to leave behind. He never did.

That might have been different, if . . .

The voice, rough and using French from the streets, came out of the darkness and broke into his thoughts. "You there—halt!"

Spinning on his heel, Paxten sprinted in the opposite direction up the Rue de Turenne, his hand pressed to his side and regrets for the past cast aside in preference for surviving the immediate present.

Alexandria traced the sobs to the dining room. The heavy chairs and the dark mahogany table had been left in the high-ceilinged room, but the candelabras and the candles had been taken and the walls had been stripped of paintings and sconces. The sobbing seemed to come from under the table.

Bending down, Alexandria glimpsed a white apron over a rocking form. "What in heavens are you doing there? Come out at once—oh, for pity's sake, do stop that crying. Diana, can you say something in French to her to have her come out?"

Standing again, Alexandria moved to a side table to search for spare candles and flint. Diana muttered something to the maid, the words hesitant but the accent true. Alexandria pressed her lips tight—why had she never paid any heed to her governess and her French lessons?

She found the stub of one half-burned taper, struggled with the flint pulled from a drawer, and finally struck a spark. Flame trembled to life as the wick caught fire. Lifting the candle, Alexandria bent to study the maid.

The woman crouched under the table, her knees pulled up to her chin. She had taken her apron away from her face. Fear had left her skin pale and her eyes enormous. Alexandria recognized Marie-Jeanne as one of the kitchen maids, a skinny girl of fifteen or so. A sweet girl, but rather slow.

"Well, why is she not coming out?" Alexandria demanded, glancing at Diana.

The young woman straightened, worry darkening her blue eyes. "She is afraid the guard will return."

"Guard? Why ever would they come here in the first place?"

In answer to the questions, a spurt of rapid French flowed from Marie-Jeanne. Alexandria bent to look under the table again. "You must come out—*tu viens ici*."

Alexandria noticed Diana wincing at such mangled French, but the maid seemed at least to recognize the voice of authority, if not the words, for she edged from under the table.

Climbing to her feet, she stared about her, clutching the white apron tied over her dark, high-waisted dress and looking rather like a rabbit who intended to bolt for her hole at the first breath of trouble.

Alexandria gave the candle to her niece, then said, "Now, let us have an explanation, if you please, Marie-Jeanne. Only in English. *Parle anglais, s'il vous plaît*."

A rapid flow of French answered, and Alexandria struggled to hold her impatience with the girl. She recognized only a few words—something about English, and Bonaparte's name came into it. Ruthlessly interrupting, Alexandria said, "But where is everyone? Diana, see if you can get some answers. I am going to make a quick tour of the house."

Taking the candle with her, she left Diana with the maid, who had started babbling again in French.

In the front hall, the candle flickered in a draft from the door, and Alexandria glanced to where the footmen now stood—Frenchmen also, for she had left her English grooms in charge of the stables here. They stood one on each side of a trunk, staring about with worried frowns.

"Never mind the luggage. I want you to search the house to see if anyone else is here," she ordered. The footmen glanced at each other and Alexandria added, "*Où est—*" She broke off, struggling for the word to add to "Where is," and then she added with a wave of her hand, "everyone?"

Understanding seemed to flicker in their eyes, for they

put down the trunk, bowed, and set off to look through the downstairs rooms.

Lifting her skirts, Alexandria went up the stairs. Gradually, the sounds of the maid's babbling and the footmen's heavy steps faded and the house seemed to fill with silence. Her throat tightened. She had never been in so empty a house—at the least, there were always servants nearby.

Her kid boots echoed loudly on the floor. The faint aroma of beeswax wafted up from the candle she held. Damp, icy cold hung in the hall.

She had no need to open doors—all stood ajar. Each room she glanced into told the same story—wild disorder, a violent search, insulting disregard for privacy or ownership. Clothing had been pulled from wardrobes and stolen away. Anything that could be carried, in fact, seemed to have been taken; even the linens from the beds had been stripped and looted.

Anger flared in her, growing stronger with each defilement she glimpsed. Who could have done such a thing? And why had not her servants, both those from England as well as the Parisians she had hired, not been here to prevent it?

At last she stopped at her own bedroom and glanced inside.

She had brought her jewels and her cosmetics with her to the château, but the clothes she had left behind were now gone. The large maple wardrobe stood open and empty. The room had been stripped of its velvet curtains and even of the carpet. The mattress had been slashed and feathers pulled out, as if someone had been searching for hidden items.

Glimpsing a fragment of something white on the bare wood, Alexandria moved into the room, her cloak, dress, and petticoats rustling. Bending down, she picked up a fragment from a china figurine. It had been a favorite—a rearing white horse, its mane flaring out and one leg lifted as if celebrating its freedom. She had treasured that figurine—for being a symbol of something she had never had.

Her fist closed on all that remained—the lone leg.

Such senseless vandalism!

She would lodge a complaint at once with the authorities. The British ambassador would . . .

Would do nothing, she realized. Lord Whitworth no longer resided in France. He could not listen to her complaints and demand results from Bonaparte's government.

A chill swept over her skin.

Turning, Alexandria left the room and ran down the stairs, the candle flickering as she hurried.

She found the maid and Diana in the main hall. Marie-Jeanne now sat on the large trunk that had been brought in by the footmen. Her eyes still seemed huge, and in the dim light her skin shone unnaturally pale, but she at least seemed to have lost that edge of hysteria, for she no longer babbled.

But then Diana turned to Alexandria, and Alexandria's heart tightened at the hint of fear in her niece's eyes. "What is it?"

Diana wet her lips, then answered. "Marie-Jeanne—she says . . . she says that England has declared war on France. Bonaparte has ordered the arrest of all English citizens. The soldiers who came here—they came for us."

Two

"That is preposterous!" Alexandria said. And then she glanced around her again and held back the rest of her protests. She had been about to say that not even Bonaparte could be so uncivilized as to order the arrest of women and children, but the man obviously allowed his troops to behave in this outrageous fashion toward civilians.

In the faint glow from the single flickering candle, she turned to stare at her niece, her thoughts as crystalline as the drops of the chandelier that hung over them in the hall. With the clarity came the sharp bite of guilt, like the clamp of teeth at her throat. She ought to have taken Diana back to England months ago, when rumors of diplomatic strain first began. Her instincts had urged caution. But she had spent so long ignoring her feelings, pushing them away, that she had done the same as she always did. She had permitted herself to be persuaded.

Heavens, how many times had she allowed that?

Lips pressed tight, she straightened. A drop of wax slid from the candle onto her glove, warming her skin through the thin leather. She ignored it. The situation required level-headed control, not hand wringing over a past that could not be changed.

Voice clipped, she asked, "When did the guards arrive? And where is everyone now?"

Turning to the maid, Diana repeated the questions in French. Marie-Jeanne returned hesitant answers, the sobs gone from her voice but her tone uncertain, as if she feared the reaction that her words might bring.

Diana listened, nodding, smiling at the girl in encouragement. She had put back the hood of her traveling cloak, and the candlelight glinted on her golden curls. Then she turned to her aunt. "Poor thing. She has no idea how long she hid under the table. It seems that the French guard burst in without even knocking just as the staff had begun dinner preparations for a meal for our return. She said that the man in command—a sergeant—seemed to think the butler was lying about our not being here and that no Englishman lived with us. He questioned everyone, and when he did not get answers he liked, he ordered the house ransacked and those who were English arrested. Everything fell into a panic then. Some fled, or at least she thinks they did. She hid under the table so they would not drag her away. She had an aunt who worked for a count and was sent to the guillotine during the Revolution."

Alexandria glanced at the maid—no wonder the girl had hidden herself. Remorse stirred in her for Fenwick and the other servants she had brought with her—they had been in her care and she had failed them.

The footmen came back into the hall, lifting empty hands as if to show the lack of anyone else in the house. Diana began to untie the strings to her cloak, and that set the maid into a new round of nearly hysterical French. *"Non. Non, Mademoiselle!"*

An outpouring of protests followed this, and when the maid seemed to run down, Alexandria asked, "What has upset her now?"

Diana turned from comforting Marie-Jeanne. "She seems to think the soldiers will come back—that it is not safe and we ought to leave at once."

"I doubt they will return tonight—we cannot be of that much interest, and I imagine they have their hands full with other English visitors." Alexandria frowned. Had the Fairchilds left Paris in time, or had they and their English staff been taken up?

She had so liked the plump and chatty Mary Fairchild. And what of the Aldersons? And the Bentleys? And a dozen others whom she had met?

She pushed aside such worries. What mattered now was to see Diana out of this. The last outbreak of hostilities had dragged on for nearly a decade. She could not risk that Diana might spend who knew how many years of her youth trapped as a prisoner of war. And she did not trust that Bonaparte would arrest only Englishmen and allow women passage home, nor that he would give his prisoners the respect due their station.

The one glimpse she had had of the man, actually, had given her the impression of a dynamic personality, but also of a man unconcerned with anyone other than himself. She certainly knew far too much about such gentlemen.

Once Diana was safe, however, she could see to her responsibilities to her servants who had been arrested. For now all that mattered was her niece.

Turning, she gave a last look at the Paris house. She had brought not just her staff with her but her china, and the good linen from home, the ones embroidered with the Sandal crest of interwoven holly and oak leaves. And she had brought some of her favorite paintings and furnishings, for she had seen no reason not to travel in comfort. Now what had not been taken already must be left behind for other thieves. But she had her jewel case in the coach—and they had the clothing that they had taken to the château. Still, they had traveled light, for it had been but a short visit.

She would hope it would also be a fast trip to the coast.

Focusing on plans helped her ignore the faint edge of fear that shivered on her skin.

Calais gave the shortest crossing of the Channel, but Dieppe lay closer to Paris. Or they could choose a port between and make for Boulogne. But first priority must be to leave Paris—if they could.

Turning her back on the nearly empty house, she ordered,

"Diana, tell Marie-Jeanne to go to the coach. We leave at once. You two, take the trunk back to the carriage—oh, they are giving me that blank look again. Diana, dear, see if you can make them understand that we are leaving Paris again."

"Do we return to the Château d'Esclimont?" Diana asked.

Alexandria shook her head. "Laval is a military man, and if orders are now indeed that all English must be detained, we cannot put him in the position of having to arrest his guests. So we shall leave as we arrived tonight—through the north gate, past Montmartre—and then start for the coast."

And they might also be better off burning their passport papers and relying more on Diana's beauty and a good amount of bribery, she thought. But she kept such plans to herself.

Then, of all the absurd things, her stomach rumbled, protesting the lack of a regular dinner. She pressed a hand to it. What a bother this was—why must these Frenchmen make everything into a grand production? In England, before such an action as this occurred, the word would have gone out through unofficial channels so that everyone could have a chance to leave in proper order. But Bonaparte, it seemed, had to make this into a theatrical display of his power. Bother the man!

Diana finished relaying the orders in French. The footmen moved forward to take the trunk back outside to the waiting coach—they would have to travel slowly to make the team last, Alexandria decided. She wanted as few stops as possible, to lessen the risk that they might be exposed as English visitors and arrested. And then the maid hurried out behind the footmen, glancing to either side as if she expected soldiers to jump from the shadows.

After snuffing her candle, Alexandria came to her niece's side and put a comforting arm around her. "Do not worry—I shall see you safe home."

"Worry?" Diana turned bright eyes to her aunt. "Why, this is the most exciting thing to ever happen! Just think—we are being swept up by history. We are in the very center of a critical juncture of fate—and we are seeing it all unfold before us. Are you certain we could not stay, perhaps there is something we could do to find Fenwick and the others and free them?"

Frowning, Alexandria took her niece's arm and steered her to the door. "What we can do is see ourselves safe—and then I shall see if I cannot at least ransom my staff through whatever channels remain open. This is all the adventure I want, thank you."

With four already fatigued horses, they made slow time in retracing their route from the city. As the carriage wheels rumbled along the ancient narrow streets, Alexandria noticed the strained silence that filled the coach. Marie-Jeanne huddled in a corner while Diana sat on the edge of her seat, peering out the window and obviously hoping for more excitement than was wise.

Alexandria battled her remorse. Would Fenwick and the others be decently housed and fed? She could not imagine they would end in the dungeons of the Bastille. But what could she do for them from England? Would she even be able to get Diana home again—or would they be imprisoned with their staff?

Pushing such thoughts away, she tried to focus on making lists of things to do. But the trick that had served her well in past years failed now.

At the city gates, the guards seemed suspicious to see a coach that had passed in the other direction only an hour before. Alexandria found her lack of mastery in the country's language frustrating, but Diana smiled, fluttered her eyelashes, and—from what Alexandria could make out from the French she understood—invented a story of sudden illness in the family.

The guards seemed reluctant to accept such a story, but after staring into the coach—which left poor Marie-Jeanne pale-faced and even more withdrawn—and muttering to each other in low voices, the gate lifted and a guard waved them through.

Alexandria let out a breath. But it still seemed a very long way to the Channel. She was glad now that they traveled in a black coach without the Sandal crest upon its doors. She had borrowed the carriage from her brother, for he had only just bought it and she had appreciated the modern steel springs and the touches of luxury he had paid for. If their luck held, the coach and Diana would be back with him within the week.

Not two miles later, their luck ran out.

Providence arrived in the form of a carriage and pair.

His side aching, Paxten ran for the slow-moving vehicle. No footman stood up behind the coach, so he caught one of the handholds and swung himself onto the back step. He clung to the swaying coach, wondering how far it might take him. The steady clop of hooves replaced that of booted feet on the cobblestone. The mist—not so heavy as to soak him but enough to dampen his hair and chill his face and hands— left him wishing for a heavy cloak at the least.

Unfortunately, the carriage did not go far.

Just the other side of the Fontaine des Innocents, the ancient vehicle turned a corner and slowed. Not wanting to wait until it halted—he did not need questions about how he came to be there in place of any footman—Paxten jumped off. Then he turned up the collar of his coat, put his head down, and started back toward the fountain.

His stride long, his side aching, he turned away from the Marais district—and General D'Aeth's mansion. He was not far from the Palais Royal, that den of sin and debauchery which housed prostitutes, gambling hells, and every other known vice. Or at least all the vices he knew. But he did not intend to stay and partake.

The diversions of the Palais Royal had barely started—the

night, and the hours for sin, had barely begun. Even so, a few gentlemen already the worse for too much drink staggered from the once-royal buildings.

Paxten watched them and settled on one portly fellow—the one who staggered the most. Following the man to the stables in the mews behind the building, Paxten waited for his chance. The smell of straw and horse filled the damp air. A thin, ragged stable boy led the portly man's horse—a sway-backed gray—to him and helped the man into the saddle with a good deal of grunting. Paxten waited in the shadows.

Sure enough, not two doors down the street, the fellow sagged as Paxten had hoped. The horse stopped and the portly man slid from the saddle and into the gutter.

With a glance behind him, Paxten slipped from the shadows and took the reins from the drunkard's loosened fingers. He started to put his foot in the iron stirrup, then glanced back at the man who lay passed out in the street.

He turned away again, then glanced down the street. What if a carriage passed this way, traveling at too fast a speed to see a body lying across the way?

Merde!

Turning from the horse, Paxten looped the reins over his arm, then bent, grabbed the fellow by the shoulders of his coat, and dragged him into a doorway. He left him propped there. He could not afford to pay the fellow anything for the horse—and the sot would probably only drink it away, he told himself—but he dug out a coin and left it in the man's pocket anyway.

Foot in the stirrup, he swung up, teeth clenched against the burning in his side. Then he grinned as he urged the horse forward with his heels. That made two commandments he had nearly broken that night. How many more would he strain or break before the dawn rose?

Giving the horse its head, he allowed it to choose its own path—so long as it was away from the general and Paris he did not care. But he wondered if D'Aeth had alerted the city gates to look for a wounded man who might be seeking escape? If the general had, then one more commandment would need to be broken—to keep his freedom, he would probably have to kill someone.

Boots clicking on the marble floor and saber rattling at his side, Captain Giles Taliaris strode away from his meeting with the general. His lieutenant, stationed at the entrance, glanced at him as Taliaris reached the tall, wide doors to General D'Aeth's mansion. The man straightened and snapped a salute. "Orders, sir?"

Taliaris's mouth tightened. He disliked the situation. He disliked his orders. He did not think highly of the general's wife, who flirted with every man she met. However, matters had gone beyond flirtation tonight. The general's honor—and that of his wife—had been tarnished. A half-English dog had taken Madame D'Aeth's coquetry for something more and had attempted to rape her.

"She was nearly hysterical when the guards came to her rescue," the general had said, his silver, military side-whiskers bristling and his plump face reddening. He had clasped his hands behind his back, and the gold braid on his elaborate uniform glinted in the candlelight. "She was naked, and—"

He broke off, almost choking on his anger. Taliaris knew better than to say anything. The general's temper had become legend to all who served under him.

Then the older man ground out, his tone savage, "Find this Marsett. Lisette said he has rooms near here. Find him and show him how we bring such English dogs to heel!"

Taliaris's scowl deepened. Odd that Madame D'Aeth would know where this man had rooms. However, he did not question his orders. He had grown up with a fervor to serve France. His dedication had brought him far, even though many considered him too young, at only twenty, for his rank.

But was it not the age of youth? Of change? Did not France need new ideals to make her the foremost of powers?

Yes, and into a nation where women-abusing filth such as this Marsett would not be tolerated.

With a nod to himself, Taliaris gave his orders. He would bring a smile back to his general, and he would avenge the honor of a Frenchwoman who had been badly used.

Lieutenant Paulin's eyes widened as he listened, and then he blurted out, "But we are not to blockade the north road as well as all the others?"

Taliaris lifted one corner of his mouth. "To snare a wolf, do you not leave open the door of the trap? We leave one road free—and then we know exactly where he must go. Have horses ready. I want guards stationed a quarter league beyond the gate, and I want to be there when this Marsett shows his face."

With a nod, Paulin hurried away to carry out the orders.

Taliaris glanced back at the D'Aeth mansion, an odd tingling between his shoulder blades. He frowned, still disliking his orders. Then he strode out of the elegant building. France was again at war with England, and so shooting this half-Englishman was nothing more than a patriotic act. So why did his skin prickle?

Pushing back his shoulders, he strode into the dark night. France could not afford soft sons—not if she were to keep her liberty and her power.

For France, he would do what he must.

It was cold, but not as cold as the Alps had been when the army of France had crossed them. And tonight's rain had stopped. So Pierre considered himself lucky to have drawn this assignment. Leaning against the white plaster wall of a cottage, he wondered what name this tiny village had. The residents had seen the uniforms and wisely bolted doors and shutters. On a raw spring night, Pierre could almost wish himself inside one of these half dozen snug buildings.

They were not far from the Porte Montmartre, the city gate, he knew, for they had marched up the road. They would probably stand here all night and then they would march back. Ah, well. What else did one do these days? Still, better a soldier than a farmer, as his father had been. The work paid well enough. Or, at least, it did most months.

With a sigh, Pierre shifted his musket so he could lean on it. The good days would soon be back again. Of course the marches could be long, but he smiled as he thought of the battlefield—the terror of it, the excitement, and the pleasure after, drinking with comrades, swapping harrowing stories, or, better still, plundering a city that had resisted siege. A soldier could take what he wanted then, be it a woman, drink, or any fancy thing that caught his eye.

Yes, far better to be fighting than standing around with nothing to do but wait.

A drop of rain fell onto Pierre's sun-hardened cheek. He glanced up at the sky. Then he looked around him at the empty square and the muddy road. Clouds parted, and a moment of silver moonlight turned the village bleak; a half dozen stone houses crowded together, one of them calling itself a tavern, though it sold nothing more than bad wine. He knew because he had bought a glass to warm himself.

Twenty-six other soldiers stood in the shadows, like him, and somewhere their lieutenant and captain waited, probably in the tavern with a fire and drink.

They were looking for a man—an injured one. He did not know why, and he did not care. It was enough to have something to do after too long of parading about Paris like toys pulled out for a little boy's amusement.

Another drop fell on his face, and Pierre shifted his stance.

At least he had had his dinner. In the field, food could be stale bread that had to be eaten on the march. Now, if only they could catch this man the captain hunted, then perhaps he could find himself a bed and a woman to go in it.

He wondered if the captain was old enough to have even

had his first woman. He grinned at the thought, and he almost called out to Henri a crude joke about the captain being too young to do more than suckle at a woman's breast. Six months serving under Taliaris made him think again.

The captain might not be inside the tavern, and might hear such a comment—and he had not looked in a mood to be amused. In fact, whoever they hunted tonight must be an unlucky bastard.

A low rumbling had him glancing up at the sky again, thinking of thunder, and then he heard the jingle of harness.

Straightening, he called a soft alert to the others—to Henri and Colmar, and that lazy Anatole. Then he hefted his musket to the ready.

As others stepped over to him to block the road, his blood quickened and his senses sharpened. He forgot the aches left by too many other battles, by age, by too many nights spent sleeping on the ground, by long marches up and down mountains and across icy rivers. He glanced at Henri and winked. He could hardly wait to be back on a real battlefield again.

The coach slowed as soon as it came into sight of the torches carried by Colmar and Anatole. Pierre lifted his musket, but the driver pulled on the reins, bringing the tired horses to an easy halt. "Too bad," Pierre muttered to Henri.

The other man glanced at him. "What did you expect? You would try to drive through more than two dozen armed men?"

Pierre grinned. He might try. Just to see if he could. Musket lowered, he moved forward with the others to surround the coach. His interest quickened as a pretty blonde leaned out the lowered window to demand, "Why do we stop? Is something wrong?"

At once, the lieutenant stepped forward and opened the carriage door. "Step out, Mademoiselle."

For a moment, the girl disappeared back into the coach. Pierre leaned closer to Henri. "Maybe she'll refuse and we'll have to drag her out, eh?"

Henri grumbled an answer about never having such luck.

As he did, the carriage door opened and the girl reappeared. She hesitated, and the lieutenant barked an order to let down the steps for her. He stared at Pierre as he spoke.

Now I'm a footman, am I? Pierre kept the complaint to himself, then he forgot about it as the girl stepped from the coach and into the torchlight.

A dark cloak covered most of her but parted to show glimpses of a figure still plump with youth. Golden curls flashed from under a bonnet with a curling feather and what looked to be silk ribbon. She had an oval face—a pretty one, Pierre could see in the flickering light, though he could not make out the color of her eyes. But what did they matter? His blood moved even faster.

Then another woman stepped out, satin rustling and bringing a faint hint of spiced perfume with her. Taller than the girl, she carried herself with the assurance of experience, and the hard angles of her face put her past any blush of youth, even though the slender figure he could glimpse under her cloak seemed young.

No meat on this one. And she thought too much of herself. She glanced around her, her straight nose up a little. She, too, wore a rich bonnet, and she made him think of the aristos years ago on the way to meet Madame Guillotine. He had been in the Revolutionary Guard back then and had been happy to see those aristos lose their proud heads. Most had had this look—this arrogant tilt to their chins, the slightly raised brows as if faintly insulted. They thought themselves better than everyone, as if they did not have to piss into a chamber pot like everyone else.

Then she looked straight at him, and he became aware of the stubble on his chin, and the wrinkles in his uniform, and that he smelled of garlic from his dinner, and that he had not bathed in a week.

He glanced away, looking back into the carriage and seeing one more shadow. "You—out! You heard the lieutenant!" he ordered.

The figure in the coach cringed, and Pierre looked at the lieutenant for permission, eager to give these too-proud women a show of real power. The lieutenant gave a nod, and Pierre leaned into the coach, grabbing for a hold on the shadowy figure and hoping he would pull out the man they sought. Maybe they would even make him a corporal again, eh?

His hand closed over a slim arm and he heard a muffled whimper, then he dragged out a small dark-haired girl.

After the golden beauty, she seemed scrawny—nothing but big eyes and a pale face. A maid, he decided, his mouth pulling down. He let go of her arm and rubbed his palm down his trouser leg as she huddled into her dark woolen cloak. The Revolution had made all of France into citizens—but the old ways crept back; those in power needed to have their boots washed for them. Better to be a farmer, even, than a servant.

Then the lieutenant started barking orders again. "Search the coach. I want every bag opened. You there, driver—step down! And you two at the back as well!"

Pierre did not wait for the driver to come down but went up after him, thrusting him from his seat. Then he climbed up to unlash the trunks on the top. The pretty blonde protested, her words shrill, but the older woman stayed oddly silent as they pushed the trunks down to the road and spilled out frothy lace and silken dresses.

Jumping down, Pierre joined the others to paw through the delicate gowns, ignoring the young woman's cries, enjoying himself now. True enough that a man might hide in one of the larger trunks, but only a dwarf could fit in these little ones. He liked the smell of the dainty silks though. It put him thinking about pawing other things.

And then a sharp voice cut through the night, snapping Pierre and the others to stiff attention. "What is this?"

Sullen now, his enjoyment gone, Pierre did not look up to meet Captain Taliaris's stare—he knew too well the sound of the captain's displeasure.

Three

The girl's shrill voice carried to him in the breath of a cold north wind as good as any alarm, and Paxten pulled hard on the reins to stop the plodding gray. Then he straightened in the saddle, trying to focus his dizzy mind.

Standing in the stirrups, he winced as the pain throbbed in his side, but he glimpsed light flickering in the darkness. From a village? Some sort of local celebration? Only that had not sounded like a woman's cry of delight.

Had someone sprung a trap set for him?

The back of his neck had started to tingle after finding the Porte de Clichy and the Porte de St. Ouen well guarded, but the Porte Montmartre had only a pair of half-asleep sentries. Why should that gate be so easy and the others wrapped as tight as a noose? Damn that city for its walls and confounded gates.

The same sense that had saved his life during the few months he had tried his hand at being a soldier of fortune, and which had served him equally well during his recent life at the gaming tables, had blared an alarm. Now he glanced again at the countryside. Should he leave the road now? His father had grown up not far from here, but he had spent his youth in England, so what chance did he have in the darkness? Might he run smack into a patrol on the hunt for him?

He settled into the saddle and urged the gray forward, thumping its fat sides with his legs to make it move. He guided the horse off the main road, cutting across a recently plowed field. The gray slogged through the mud.

As he neared the village, the flickering light resolved into torchlight. Within its glow, he could make out what looked to be a few cottages. And a carriage? Yes, a carriage—he could see the horses shift uneasily in their harness. Then he glimpsed a flash of fire on metal and he reined in the gray. His service for the King of Naples had taught him to recognize the glint of a bayonet.

Soldiers.

A number of them, he judged by the thump of boots he could now hear and the clipped tone of orders being issued. He glanced at the darkness around him. Did others wait nearby, spread out across the countryside?

Merde!

Instinct urged him to turn the gray and find out if the beast had a gallop in it, to leave the road and this village far behind. But he forced himself to take a breath and calculate the odds of this nag being able to outpace mounted cavalry.

Not a bet he really wanted to take, he decided.

He might have risked it if he weren't bleeding and already swaying in the saddle.

And then he grinned. If he could not run, then why not see if he could find a safer route? One that might take him under their noses. He had the advantage, after all, in that he knew where they were. But they had not seen him. Could he keep it so?

Swinging out of the saddle, his boots hit the mud with a soft squelch. The world spun and his knees buckled. Pressing his hand to his side, he leaned against the horse to catch his breath. Mother of mercy, he needed to get someplace where he could rest and tend his wound. He would just have to hope his instincts were right about this.

Straightening, he stepped away from the gray. It stood there a moment, staring at him, so he turned its head and slapped its rump to set it ambling back to Paris. Then, stepping as silently as he could with mud sucking at his boots, he moved toward the village.

Furious now, Diana shrieked at the soldiers to stop vandalizing their property. She grabbed her chemise from one thick-set lout and spun to snatch her aunt's jewelry box from another. And then a sharp voice had the soldiers dropping anything they held—gowns, shawls, bonnets—and snapping to stiff attention.

Rather than stepping forward to pick up their garments, Marie-Jeanne huddled in the background, but Diana caught a muttered word from her aunt. *"Ordure!"*

Diana almost smiled. Trash. The word could be applied to the clothes now strewn in the mud or to these idiots who had ruined their garments. She suspected her aunt intended the latter.

Then the soldiers stepped back to allow another man to come forward, and she turned to him, her anger hot and leaving her French stuttering. "Who is in charge here? Why have we been stopped? This is an outrage—I assure you that my aunt's friend, the Duke of Laval, shall hear about . . ."

And then her words faded as the man stepped fully into the circle of torchlight.

The light turned sun-darkened skin into shadows of bronze. Tall, square-faced, and broad, he looked the perfect military man. His dark-blue uniform emphasized his wide shoulders. Tall black boots gleamed in the firelight, and the gold braid on his chest flashed. A red dolman swung from his shoulders.

She stared at him. Dark brows angled over deep-set eyes. A saber rattled at his side, and he stood with one hand braced on the sword hilt as he glanced around at his men and the disorder they had created.

Then he looked at her, and Diana realized she must seem ridiculous with her mouth partly open and her bonnet askew and her chemise caught up to her chest and clutching her aunt's jewel box.

She hid her silk chemise behind her. "Are you in charge of this rabble?"

With a shallow bow, he said, his voice a pleasant tenor that made her wonder if he was younger than she had first thought, "Captain Giles Taliaris at your service, Mademoiselle . . . ?"

His trailing words invited an answer. Ought she give him her own name, or did Edgcot sound too English?

Aunt Alexandria solved the problem by stepping forward and muttering from behind a handkerchief, as if she were ill, "I feel unwell."

The handkerchief muffled her aunt's too-English accent, and Diana did the rest, clutching her aunt's swaying form as if she feared an immediate collapse. Then she turned her best smile on the captain, and hoped he might be more stupid than he looked.

"I beg your pardon, Captain, but my aunt, she is not well. I must get her to a doctor in . . . in Calais."

His stare did not leave her face. "You seem uncertain of your destination."

She started to frown at him, caught herself, and lowered her lashes instead. "Yes, I am so stupid about such things. That is why our driver knows the direction. And I must get my aunt there at once." She looked up, striving for a stricken look. Only she was not much of an actress. She had barely muddled through being Juliet in her aunt's house party last year when they had done Shakespeare's tragedy. This looked as if it might have an equally sad end.

"We fear it is consumption," she said, her voice low.

A few soldiers shuffled away, putting their hands to their mouths, left uneasy by an illness that had no cure and left one coughing up blood and slowly wasting away.

The captain, however, only glanced at Diana's aunt, his face expressionless. Then he looked back at Diana. For a moment, the torchlight shifted and she caught a glimpse of his eyes. Brown eyes—a mix of warm and dark. Shrewd intelligence flashed in the depths.

He knew the truth.

The color drained from her face, leaving her skin colder than the raw spring night warranted. *How did he know?* Had he guessed? Or had she given them away somehow by overplaying her role?

Heart beating fast, she met his stare, her eyes wide and the truth now in her mind, willing him to understand. *We just want to go home. We are no harm to anyone.*

It seemed forever that he stared at her, his dark eyes again shadowed, his stern features revealing nothing of his thoughts. The pulse pounded sluggish in Diana's throat. Once. Twice. Three times. She counted each beat. Would he arrest them now?

Then he turned to face the man who had ordered them from the coach, a short, lean man with pox scars on his cheeks. "The man we want is not here—pack the mademoiselle's and the madame's trunks. They are to go on their way at once."

Glancing at her aunt, Diana let out a long breath. Her aunt seemed to have caught enough of what was said to have grasped that they were to go. *Aller.*

Diana turned to the captain again. "Thank you," she said, putting all the feeling she could into the words. *"Merci beaucoup."*

His mouth lifted in the faintest of smiles, and she realized he had an attractive face—and an even more attractive mouth, with a full lower lip.

She smiled back.

Then his face hardened again and he said, his voice pitched only for her and her aunt, "You may find it best for your aunt's health to take her farther than Calais. I urge a sea voyage. France is not the place for two ladies who have no protection beyond their own reckless courage."

Stiffening, Diana started to deny they had ever been reckless about anything, but her aunt squeezed her arm tight, silencing her.

He turned away, all brusque military bearing as he barked orders to his men, sending some scurrying into the darkness while the rest finished a hasty repacking of the ruined clothes.

Diana glanced around, her brows pulled tight and an odd hollowness in her. An easing perhaps of the tension of a moment ago? Yes, partly that, she knew. But his remark had stung—he could have at least acknowledged her thanks!

Well, she would be glad that he had allowed them to leave, even though he seemed to suspect that they were not French. But considering what he had said about their carriage not holding the man they wanted, perhaps the captain's gallantry was nothing more than a desire not to be distracted from his duty by mere women.

That rankled even more.

And then she realized that she still held her chemise and her aunt's jewel box as well as her aunt's arm. Turning slowly, as if with a care for her aunt's health, Diana led her back to the coach, leaning close to whisper in English, "I think he knows—"

Her aunt interrupted, her tone sharp and her French halting. "Hush—not here."

Diana nodded, her cheeks hot. She did not seem to be very good at this pretending, and that endangered them all.

At the coach, Marie-Jeanne shifted from one foot to the other. "May I be excused, Madame. For a moment only. Nature calls."

Diana stared at the maid, and then realized that the girl needed to visit the privy. She could not blame the girl, her own insides had almost gone liquid. Her aunt nodded to the maid, then said in her poor French, "Hurry back."

After one frightened glance at the soldiers, Marie-Jeanne put her head down and lifted her skirts to pick a path around the nearest house and to whatever facilities might exist behind it.

To maintain the pretense that her aunt was ill, Diana made a show of helping her into the coach. After seeing her chemise and her aunt's jewel case repacked, she got into the coach herself. With the driver back in his seat, the luggage strapped to the roof again, and the footmen both shifting nervously beside the door, Diana called out, "Marie-Jeanne?"

The soldiers seemed to have lost interest in them, for they sauntered away, taking the torchlight with them. The night seemed darker. Moonlight crept out, then vanished as the clouds parted and then thickened, pushed by the sharp wind.

Diana started to call the girl's name again, but then she heard hurrying footsteps and the flap of skirts. The moon slipped out from the clouds again, and Diana glimpsed the maid, the hood of her cloak pulled up and her skirts fluttering as she strode toward the coach.

The maid struggled for a moment with her skirts and the steps of the coach, but then she flung herself inside the coach and huddled in a dark corner. Hurrying, the footman put up the steps and shut the door. The driver cracked his whip and the carriage lurched forward, the team having to drag the wheels loose from the mud.

"What took you so long?" Diana asked.

Marie-Jeanne gave no answer but only pressed herself deeper into the corner of the coach.

Suddenly uneasy, Diana stared at the maid.

But her aunt's voice, calm as ever, drew Diana's attention. "I pray that is as close a call as we have for the rest of this trip. But since you mentioned Calais, I think we will do better now to make for Boulogne—just in case that captain changes his mind about us. The trick now will be to find a change of horses."

Between the mud and the tired horses, it took them two hours to cover the next ten miles. They found an inn willing to open and offer them food and a fresh team for hire. The candles in the lanterns set on either side of the carriage doors had burned out, and Alexandria decided not to replace them. Somehow it seemed better to draw the least notice possible.

Diana tried to coax Marie-Jeanne from the coach to eat with them, but the maid only shook her head and shrank back into the inky corner. Poor girl—she must still be fretting over the soldiers, Alexandria decided, and let her be.

Twenty minutes later she and Diana stepped back into the coach, having eaten quickly. The grooms already had fresh horses in harness, so as soon as the door was shut the coach started forward at a brisk pace.

Marie-Jeanne seemed to be asleep, but Diana leaned forward, offering a slice of lamb on bread. "Marie-Jeanne, I brought you something to eat."

The maid said nothing.

"Leave her to sleep," Alexandria urged, swaying with the coach's motion.

"Oh, but she must be hungry." Leaning forward, Diana took hold of the maid's leg to wake her. She pulled back at once, dropping the lamb. "You're not Marie-Jeanne!"

A low purr of a masculine voice answered in English, "No, I am not. But I do have a gun pointed at you, so I advise you not to do anything foolish."

Four

Alexandria stared at the shadowy figure across from her, shock cold on her skin. Fatigue blunted her thoughts and her feelings, but not so much that she could not recognize that voice. Her pulse quickened and her throat dried. Impossible that it should be him, appearing as if summoned by her earlier thoughts.

And yet . . . excitement shimmered. Could it be? Oh, to see him again, after so long.

She straightened and scolded herself for her heart leaping ahead of her.

Still, she narrowed her eyes, trying to make out his features, trying to be certain, willing herself to be mistaken, and her hands quivering that she might be. She wished she did not feel young and eager again. Age ought to bring more than wrinkles. Yet, she knew the truth. Knew it in ways that had nothing to do with the rational mind.

Her skin vibrated with the awareness of him. His voice had always done that to her—that languid, velvet voice still brushed across her like thick silk. It was him. The years could not change that deep knowing.

Oh, she ought to hate him for doing this to her, she decided. She had once spent hours picturing their meeting again—at some social function, in a park perhaps—but in all her fantasies she had been self-possessed, a woman of the world and no longer such a raw girl who stumbled over her words and choked on her emotions. And he had been—well, he had not been this dark, disturbing figure.

Since she had no real idea what to do, she did what she had learned to do over the long years to mask her inadequacies; she resorted to sarcasm. "Paxten Marsett—how very like you to appear where you are least wanted and of no use whatsoever."

For a moment, he did not reply, and then a low, warm laugh filled the coach. "And how very like you to cross my path when you are in deeper waters than you can navigate, my Lady Scandal."

Her hands clenched on the muslin of her dress. "Do not call me that!"

"What, did I say *scandal* instead of Sandal? Old habit, I fear. But the name fits you so much better."

A light voice interrupted. "And just why do you think my aunt scandalous, when you are the one threatening us?"

Diana's words startled Alexandria. She had focused her attention so totally on Paxten that she had forgotten everything else. As she almost had once before. She glanced at her niece, then turned back to blister Paxten with a reproof for the use of that sobriquet he had once given her, and which he had lured her into earning.

However, he got his words out before she could utter hers, that charm of his now turned on Diana. "Aunt, is it? How do you do? Since your aunt has already given you my name, that must do for an introduction. And you are . . . ?"

Voice prim, Diana answered without hesitation, "I doubt I should give you my name—it does not sound as if Aunt Alexandria cares overmuch for you."

Proud of the girl, Alexandria smiled. She wished she had had one-tenth of Diana's pert arrogance ten years ago. As the carriage rocked, she glanced back toward Paxten.

Then he said, his voice so soft it almost did not carry over the muffled sounds of the horse's steady trot, "Oh, she once cared for me—or so I thought."

Throat tight, Alexandria stared at him. Was he mocking her? Making light of what she had indeed once felt for him?

Her anger flared and she lashed out, "Really, Paxten, I thought you at least beyond hiding behind a woman's skirts. What did you do with poor Marie-Jeanne?"

"Your little maid? Well, she is a touch less poor—she had the last of my coins for her cloak and skirt."

"And, of course, she gave her garments to you quite willingly?" Alexandria said, hoping the doubt in her tone scalded him.

"Oh, my touch has much improved for getting a woman out of her clothes."

Alexandria's hands clenched again. "So has your knack for leaving a lady in distress, it seems. Just where did you leave her?" She sat straighter. "You did not harm her, did you?"

Irritation hardened his tone. "What do you take me for?"

"I take you for a rogue who would carry off a girl's clothes!"

"Well, I am that—but it was her clothes or my life, and I'm rather more attached to the latter than she was to the former."

As if unable to hold back the question, Diana asked, "Your life? Are you the wounded man those soldiers are hunting?"

Alexandria sat up, tension now coiled in her. "Wounded? And you have the effrontery to accuse me of being in deeper waters than I can navigate. Where are you injured?"

That languid tone of his took on a clipped sharpness. "Have a mind to your own cares, my lady. I overheard those soldiers. France is not a happy place for any Englishwoman just now, and here you two are, parading about as if it were five o'clock in Hyde Park! It may actually be good fortune that has brought us together."

"I doubt that! And our parading has so far managed to keep us safe, which is more than you have managed."

"It's only a scrape."

"In that case, you will not mind walking to the next village. Diana, lower the window and tell the—"

A rapid flow of harsh French cut off Alexandria's words. *"Tiens! C'est toujours la même rengaine!"*

Not understanding, she scowled at him in the gloom. Then Diana asked, "What does he mean, it is always the same story?"

Shifting in his seat to ease the ache in his side, Paxten allowed the question to hang a moment. So the little one knew more of the language than did her aunt. Well, it still seemed unlikely that such a skill would get these two as far as they needed to go. Nor as far as he needed.

"The story of your aunt and I," he told her. Then he glanced at the woman he had once known so well, seeing no more than a pale face, indistinct in the moonlight. It seemed that their story had not ended. He smiled. "Relax, my Lady Scandal. If I'd known this was your coach, I would not have invited myself along, but since I am here, we may as well make use of each other."

Her answer came at once, as cool as only an English voice could be. "I have no use for you, Mr. Marsett."

He smiled. He could imagine her expression—elegant eyebrows arched, gray eyes chill as a morning mist, that lovely mouth of hers prim. He always wanted to kiss her when she took on that look—to ruffle her into losing those airs of hers. She still stirred that inclination, but he had not the energy to act on it just now.

However, he knew other ways to rattle that facade of hers.

With a smile, he spoke in French, his accent that of the streets. Now he would see just how much the niece knew. "One musket ball across my ribs is all I care for tonight, Madame. And there are miles to put between Paris and myself if I am to be certain there won't be more. You ought to sympathize with that. So, since we both wish to depart this land, why do we not join forces? You'll need someone to bargain for your passage across the Channel if you do not wish your pretty throat—and that of your niece—slit to gain your jewels. And I need—I need transport as well."

The rest of his needs he could ignore. For now.

He could not see her expression, but he could imagine her glowering at him, frustrated with him and wishing to wring his neck. He glanced at the niece, another pale face, with moonlight glinting on pale curls. Then Alexandria leaned over to her niece for a hushed consultation. He heard the girl mutter, "I only caught something about jewels and leaving France and needing your help."

He chuckled, then said, "No, *ma fille,* it was my help that I am offering to get you to England."

"In exchange for my jewels?" Alexandria asked, her tone sharp.

Her assumption irritated him, but he had not fully decided yet how to play this next act between them, so he only said, "Terms are yet negotiable. However, let us start by saying that my immediate need of you just now is fast conveyance. And in exchange, perhaps I can assist you with what it is you wish to gain."

The carriage swayed around a bend in the road, forcing him to lean into the turn. Pain shot up his side as he did, and he winced and muttered a soft oath.

Fabric rustled as Alexandria half rose and then shifted to sit next to him. "Bother you, Paxten! Now I wish I had left the lanterns lit. Just how little is this scrape of yours?"

He frowned as she pulled off her gloves, her white hands appearing so slim and pale in the moonlight. Disapproval radiated from her as palpable as the warmth from her body, but a familiar scent of vanilla and spice teased to life memories of his arms around her, of soft lips, of how she tasted.

She stripped them away with crisp questions shot at him as if she were his nursemaid. "Just what did you manage to have scraped? Your leg? Arm? Side? Have you broken anything?"

Soft hands began to search over him, and he frowned. He did not like the sensations she stirred—no, he would not allow her ever again to leave him vulnerable to her touch.

Taking her hands, he pushed them away. "There is no need for you to poke at me as if you were some healer."

"Oh, for—this is my brother's coach and I do not wish your

blood to stain it. Besides, how much help will you be if you bleed to death? Now, stop being so stupid about this."

"You are the bothersome one, you know. You always were. Very well, if you must, then fuss. Here, now, Aunt Alexandria's niece, you may pull off my skirts, for I had the dress caught up around my waist only for show. If your aunt wishes to wrap me in soft muslin, they'll do well enough to do so."

Her tone stiff—imitating her aunt, he decided—the girl said, "You may call me Miss Edgcot."

Paxten stared into the darkness at her, amused. Fabric rustled as the girl tugged Marie-Jeanne's skirts from his white breeches and black boots. "You have an edge to you, *ma fille,* but not so soft as on a cot. And I shall call you Miss Stuffy if you use such a tone as that—what are you teaching the girl, Andria?"

Beside him, Alexandria stiffened. Did she object to his use of his own pet name for her? And where had that sprung from? He had promised himself ten years ago to keep his distance from her, and women like her—proper ladies. Yet, here he was, already falling into old, easy habits with her. *Merde*—perhaps he ought to have her stop the coach and set him down.

Then she said, "I hope I am teaching her to be wise and thoughtful, and polite."

He had to laugh, and his side ached for it, sobering him. He had forgotten how she could make him laugh. "That sounds unconscionably dull," he told her.

"I am not dull!" The girl's indignant reply came at once, followed by a ripping of fabric. Did she have his skin in mind now as she tore? He grinned.

Alexandria took the fluttering strip of fabric. "A little more dullness, Mr. Marsett, and you would not be sitting here bleeding. Now please open your cloak and your shirt."

Voice dropping lower, he whispered to her, "For you, that is always a pleasure."

She said nothing, but he could feel her bristling beside

him. Ah, why did he do this? She brought out the worst in him, made him want to bedevil her, to drive her until she lost her control. But he had never been able to make her forget herself completely. Was that not their tragedy?

He frowned at her now as he remembered again. He still had not forgiven her. The anger still burned. She had condemned them both to this inadequate existence. But, for her, it seemed not so bad. Yes, Lady Scandal's life went on rather better. Even in the gloom he could see the jewels sparkle at her ears and her throat. The richness of her coach comforted him.

He could hate her.

He would have to—or go mad.

With a muffled curse, he untied the strings at the throat of the black cloak he had taken from the wide-eyed maid. He had left his coat at the village, taking the maid's dress so that he could step into it and hold it around his waist, letting the skirts—not his boots and breeches—show under the cloak's hem as he made for the coach.

Wincing now, he pulled the matted, wet fabric of his shirt from his skin. Blood-wetted skin. *Merde,* he had been bleeding again.

Alexandria drew in a sharp breath. "You need a doctor."

"I need a large brandy and a stop in a soft bed."

Alexandria's niece ripped off another strip of fabric. And then soft hands pressed a pad of folded fabric against his skin. White dots danced before his eyes. He leaned his head back and shut his eyes, letting Alexandria's voice recede into the distance. "Drink will get you a fever. And if you stop for long, you are likely to be taken up for . . . just what did you do to . . . no, I do not want to know what you did to be shot. Please sit up so I can bind this now."

It took focused effort to obey her, but he managed to push himself up by bracing his left hand against the seat. Cool fingers brushed his skin as she wound the strip of gown around him, and that scent of hers teased him again as she leaned closer. That light touch stirred his anger—and his desire.

He started talking nonsense to distract himself from that touch. "But, *ma chère,* I might have been shot for something dashing and romantic—spying for England, even."

Miss Edgcot stopped tearing fabric and asked, awe and curiosity mixed in her voice, "Were you?"

He had to smile at that—so young, so gullible. As he had once been. Alexandria's cool answer, however, carried the weight of one far more jaded. "Mr. Marsett was ever too idealistic for anything so politic as spy work."

Her words dug into him. *Idealistic*—she said it as if it were a malady to hide in shame. Well, she had cured him of that ailment. But it irritated him that she thought she knew him so very well. Ah, she knew nothing. Not of him at least.

"What makes you think I have not changed?" he asked, his tone casual.

For a moment she held still. Her cloak had fallen open and he could see the white skin of her throat, and the quick rise and fall of her breasts. Lovely breasts, soft and pale and delicious.

That insidious tug of attraction pulled him to her. After all these years, after the bitter parting, after all she had done to him, he still wanted her. Did she feel it too? Did it coil inside her, this urge to touch, this need to taste, this craving to possess? Or had that aching desire long ago died in her?

Voice as calm as ever, she asked, "Do any of us ever really change all that much?"

His mouth crooked. He had changed—she had done that to him. His eyes narrowed. If he had been alone with her, he might have taken her throat in his hands—or he might have done other things to her. His mouth lifted at one corner. That assumed, of course, that he actually could do anything given his present condition.

Still, he wanted now to see if he could tear open her heart as she had once done to him. And this time, might she be the one seduced and then cast aside? A sweet thought, that one. He let it linger.

Hands fumbling, she finished knotting the ends of the makeshift bandage. "That will do."

"Yes, yes, it will," he agreed. Her chin rose and he felt her stare on him, searching in the darkness to see him.

The carriage hit a rut in the road, jostling him, throwing him back against the leather squabs. It threw Alexandria against him, and he caught her, partly so that she would not land against the gash in his side and partly because he ached to have his hands on her.

His fingers tightened around her arms, and he held her. Long enough to feel her softness give under his grip. Long enough to hear the ragged breath that trembled in her. Long enough for the heat from her face to warm his.

He smiled as the pulse fluttered in her wrists. So she still could not be honest with him. While her voice might lie with its scorn, her body could not. She gave to him—gave as he had dreamed of on far too many nights. But it was not enough.

This time he was no idealistic youth caught with his heart in his first love. This time he knew how to seduce a woman—even a woman such as her. This time he could use his skills against her.

Pulling away from him, she fled to the other side of the coach. He let her go. He had time yet. And more than a hundred miles to the coast of France.

Shutting his eyes, he relaxed. "The world always changes, and not always for the better, my Lady Scandal."

He had spoken in French, muttering something. Alexandria understood only a little of it, and that he had used that much-hated name for her.

However, it was his tone that chilled her. So empty. So hard. She turned away to stare out the coach window at nothing but darkness. The man she had known had never spoken in such a voice. She shivered and began to smooth on her gloves again. She traveled, it seemed, not with a man she had known but with a stranger. Her heart tightened.

It was not wise to even consider traveling with him. Yet,

she had to think of Diana. Paxten could pass himself off as a native—his father had been one after all. That might well speed their journey home. But she also remembered him as a man who put himself and his pleasures first. He never had given any thought to consequences or duty. Did that argue well for Diana's safety?

Putting a hand up, she rubbed her forehead. She did not have to decide anything at this instant. She could think better in the morning, when they stopped again for food and fresh horses. Yes, that would do. After all, she could not very well put him down on the road in the middle of the night, though that might be wiser.

She had never been very wise with him.

After taking off her bonnet, she closed her eyes and leaned her head against the corner of the coach, hoping for sleep. But her fingertips tingled—how good it had been even to skim her fingers across his skin. She kept seeing his shirt fall open to show that broad, muscular chest. Her mouth dried.

Then her chest tightened. She shifted in her seat. He had made light of the injury, but she had seen the blood on his side. What if infection set in? Or . . . *oh, stop cosseting the man!* If he said he needed only a soft bed and drink, she ought to see him to some locale where he could get them. Then they could part ways again. That would no doubt be best for everyone.

Only she could not bear the thought of it.

Opening her eyes, she stared into the darkness again.

Why must their paths cross now? And why must they part again so soon? But she knew the answer. Knew it because she had felt it shimmering around him—he hated her. And, God forgive her, perhaps she deserved it.

Sunlight brushed her eyelids, and the slowing of the coach pulled Alexandria awake. Straightening, she touched a hand to an aching neck. Her hair must look frightful. She glanced at her niece to see if she still slept.

Diana had not taken off her bonnet, and now she lay with it pushed to one side. In the pale dawn, she looked lovely, her skin soft, dark lashes resting against her cheeks, her golden curls tumbled and loose. Alexandria ran a hand over her face, certain she had added new lines to it last night. Well, that could not be helped.

Quietly, she stretched and avoided looking at Paxten. The dawn lay soft on the green countryside. Heads down, black-and-white cows grazed in a pasture. A flock of dark birds winged across the sky. The peaceful scenery made last night—with its ruined house and soldiers and hasty flight—seem unreal.

But then a booted foot brushed against hers, drawing her stare to the boot and then upward to the man seated across from her.

He lay on his side, his long, muscular legs spilling off the seat. His shirt had twisted and pulled open to show enough of him above the bandage that her pulse quickened. She ought to look away and not stare at the corded muscles of his neck or at the glimpse of broad chest visible over those crooked bandages.

Face warm, she looked away, then looked back, telling herself that she had to ensure he was not still bleeding.

Her bandages seemed to have held, for only his shirt showed the dark brown of dried blood. The ragged blue strips of fabric wound around his middle looked untidy.

How could a man be so disheveled and so attractive?

His foot brushed hers again as the coach slowed.

And then his eyes opened and his dark stare locked on hers.

Heat washed up her chest and into her cheeks. Still, she stared back. Rude of her. Rude of him to watch her in return, those liquid brown eyes so devastating with their unnerving intensity.

She parted her lips to say something—something trivial and polite. Only the words lodged in her chest in a sharp ache. If she uttered anything, it would be something foolish, such as *Why did you not come back?*

She did not voice the question. He might answer with a truth that she did not want to hear.

Mastering herself, she gave him a slight nod. He continued to stare, and she remembered the first time they had met. He had stared at her then, stared at her from across a table at which a hundred dined, making her feel foolish, and ridiculously feminine for being able to be so fascinating. Thankfully, she was beyond wanting such attention from him now.

She turned away, making the movement deliberate. She had to straighten her shoulders to keep from looking back at him.

The driver had turned off the main road and the carriage now rolled down a narrow lane toward a small village. Smoke rose from the chimneys of a dozen buildings. She would think of hot bread. Yes, and of tea. What would she not give for a hot cup of Bohea? She would not think of him. And of those dark, knowing eyes. Nor of the rush of pleasure it gave her to look into them again.

Twisting in her seat, she decided that when she did reach home again, she would have a proper traveling chaise built. That was a better thing to think about. She would plan such a carriage. One with seats that folded out to a bed.

The image followed at once—her and Paxten lying in such a bed, the carriage rocking them in each other's arms. Heat rushed through her again in a frantic flush. She did not look at Paxten for fear he would see in her eyes that image, that he would know where her thoughts of him had gone.

As they passed into the village, the carriage began to slow. Dogs chased out into the dirt road, barking shrill, with more energy than real threat.

Suddenly, Alexandria wanted out of the coach. She

wanted to stretch her legs and use whatever facilities might be available. It would be heaven to wash her face. And she wanted to be away from Paxten. How could he start to dismantle all her poise, all her defenses, with a glance? She could not allow that. She needed time to gather her wits. A few moments to remind herself that she was Lady Sandal—a respectable woman with a grown son and far beyond the age of foolishness now.

Turning, she roused Diana with a shake. "My dear, do wake. We shall stop for breakfast."

Eyes closed, Diana mumbled, "What? What is it?"

"It is dawn, and we are . . . I have no idea where we are. My dear, do wake."

Paxten's voice, low and lazy, vibrated on Alexandria's skin. "Leave the *fille* to slumber yet. The sun will still come up as it must."

Alexandria risked a glance at him and saw that he no longer lay across the seat but sat straight, and he no longer stared at her with that simmering intensity in his eyes. His expression seemed shuttered now, masked with a cynical weariness. Or perhaps just fatigue. She frowned. He did look pale—too pale.

As she watched him, his smile twisted and he asked, "Shall I order food? And rooms where you may wash and change? We must be miles from Paris, so a short rest can do no harm. But we shall have to make up some story to explain my battered state."

"Perhaps a duel over another man's wife?" Alexandria suggested, her tone dry. His eyes narrowed a fraction, and she caught her lower lip with her teeth. So she had guessed right—a woman had been involved.

Jealousy cut sharp through her, and she fought it down, telling herself over and over that she had given away any say in his life years ago. But the thought seemed not to have any connection to her feelings.

Paxten seemed not to notice her inner turmoil, for he only

crooked his mouth, then said, "Ah, but how can I be fighting duels when you are now Madame Marsett—oh, don't frown. If you do, you won't look like the dutiful and silent wife."

"Then I shall be the sister—the one who disapproves of you." She turned from him. "Diana, do wake, please. We must send one of the footmen back to see about Marie-Jeanne, to ensure she is at least returned to Paris and her family."

Yawning, Diana sat up and pushed her bonnet straight. The carriage stopped, and Paxten muttered something, and then he hauled himself up and swung out the door. He stood there, swaying for a moment, then let down the steps and offered one hand to Diana, saying something in French. Diana pinked as if flattered, but she took his hand and stepped from the coach.

Alexandria frowned as Paxten held his hand to her, his French so deliberate that even she could understand. "Do you stay in the coach all day, my sweet sister."

He drawled the word for *sister* so that it came out a caress—*suhr*. A soft endearment. She struggled for some answer in French, then gave it up and simply glared. But she gave him her hand.

His grip held more strength than she would have credited, and when she stood next to him, she glanced at him, prepared to give him a curt thank-you. She forgot the words as she glanced at him.

He looked more than exhausted. Pale skin pulled tight across high cheekbones. A day's growth of beard darkened his jaw, making him look disreputable and unfairly handsome. His gaze had become unfocused. Worried, she touched a gloved hand to his shoulder.

He glanced at her. The breeze ruffled his hair. Then he muttered something in French and with black eyelashes fluttering closed, fainted to the ground.

Five

She grabbed for him but only caught his shirt, doing little to break his fall, and then she was on her knees beside him, tearing at her gloves so that she could put a hand to his face. "Paxten! Paxten?"

His skin burned. She wanted to kick him for being so careless with himself. She wanted to scold him for terrifying her. Instead, she put a shaking hand to her head and struggled for something sensible to do. A doctor. She had told him he needed a doctor.

Straightening, one hand still on his chest, she called out, her words halting as she struggled with the language, *"Ici, s'il vous plaît! J'ai besoin d'un médecin."*

Would a village this small even have a doctor?

Her words drew stares from the coach driver and a dark-haired, portly man with an apron tied around his wide middle and a tan vest open over a crisp white shirt. The portly man—the innkeeper, she decided—said something to a slack-jawed stable boy, cuffed the lad to get him moving, and then hurried forward.

It took the coach driver and the innkeeper to carry Paxten into the inn, up the stairs, and lay him onto a bed. Alexandria followed, biting on her lower lip to keep back the flow of English words that she wanted to babble at them.

I shall learn French after this—or, better still, I shall remain in England, where I belong.

She understood enough of the innkeeper's rough country

dialect to grasp that he had sent the stable boy to the next
town to fetch the nearest surgeon. Then, with Paxten stretched
out on a narrow bed in a small bedchamber tucked under the
roof eaves, the landlord turned and urged her to leave. She
grasped that he did not think it proper for her to be present as
they undressed Paxten. She agreed. Still, she hated to go, and
from the doorway, she paused to glance back at him.

Thankfully, he wore his boots loose enough that they
slipped off with no more than a gentle pull from the coachman. The bloodstained shirt came off even more easily,
sliding off his limp body as the landlord held him up in
the bed and the coachman dragged off the ruined garment.
Paxten's head angled to the side as the landlord held him.

Alexandria's heart tightened.

Hard enough to live in a world in which she could not see
his face every day. Impossible to imagine one in which he did
not exist.

She gripped the doorjamb. *I must stop making this into a
disaster—it is only that he has lost so much blood.* But her
fingers tingled with a reminder of how hot his skin had been.
Bertram had died of such a fever after his shooting accident.

She shut the memory away.

The landlord laid Paxten's unconscious form down again,
and the coachman started to undo the buttons to Paxten's
breeches. Alexandria fled.

At the bottom of the stairs she stopped again, to think, to try
to plan. She could not imagine that Paxten might continue on
with them today. Perhaps not even for a few more days. And
that put them all in danger. Still, what choice did she have now?

But this was not her decision alone, she knew.

Diana came in a moment later, smiling brightly. "I sent
Armand back to Paris—oh, I ought to speak French only,
but . . . what is it? What is wrong?

Catching her niece's hand, Alexandria led the girl into a small
parlor. Like the rest of the inn she had seen so far, the woodwork
gleamed with polish, as did the few pieces of simple wood fur-

nishings. White curtains framed a window that overlooked the front of the inn, and wildflowers tucked into a blue pottery jug on a table splashed color into the room. Absurd to notice such details now. But it calmed her to list them in her mind.

Sitting down on a wooden settee that stood next to the unlit hearth, she tugged on Diana's hand so that her niece sat beside her.

I must be rational about this. Only how did one turn jumbled fears into any kind of sensible order?

Wetting her lips, she started to explain. "Paxten—Mr. Marsett, he fainted. Bother! That makes it sound as if he were a London miss at a first ball—he is upstairs, unconscious. And burning with fever. I . . . my dear, I cannot leave him like this. Not until I know if he will—"

She choked off the words. She could not say them. Could not give any possible reality to something she did not want to happen.

Diana frowned, her smooth forehead now bunched tight, the arches of her eyebrows tugged flat. "Of course we cannot leave."

"No, you must go on. Your safety—"

"—Is your responsibility. Yes, yes, I know. I certainly heard you promise Father too many times how you would look after me on this trip. But if you send me on alone, that is hardly looking after me, now, is it? And if you try to, I shall simply not go. I could not leave you—or Mr. Marsett, for that matter."

Folding her hands on her lap, Diana stared at her aunt. Everyone seemed to think that blond curls, a pretty face, and only seventeen years in this world meant a lack of sense. She wrinkled her nose. Her own fault, probably, for being lazy enough to always take the easiest course. Which meant being a dutiful daughter, and niece, and . . . and, oh, she was not about to be sheltered from what might be the only real adventure of her life.

Her aunt had on her steely gaze, gray eyes flat, lips pressed tight, slight frown wrinkling her forehead. Diana lifted her chin. She could withstand her aunt's glare, for she knew how deep an affection lay behind it.

Then her aunt rose to pace across the room. "No, I suppose I cannot send you off on your own. But I cannot risk you. Only, if we leave Mr. Marsett—"

"Leave him?" Diana leapt up. "As you just said, we cannot leave the poor man here with . . . with strangers. I mean—" She bit her lower lip. She must have a care. She had felt the tension between Mr. Marsett and her aunt. She had also heard a good deal in what they had not said to each other. And she was not about to see her aunt abandon such an intriguing man.

Of course, it would be sensible to do so, but being sensible never got one into any exploits.

"If you left him, you would never forgive yourself. Nor could I—forgive myself, that is, for I could not blame you if you were thinking first of me. But if you are thinking of me, then think of how it would scar my young soul to abandon someone who is obviously quite well known to you—"

"Years ago, I knew him. No longer."

"Still, that must count, must it not? Even if he were a stranger, we still could not abandon him. That would be heartless. There is the story of the Good Samaritan, after all, to serve as our example."

"As I recall, the Samaritan was not attempting to flee a hostile country."

Diana caught her aunt's hand. "But you know I am right. Besides, we are well out of Paris. And we could use a rest, could we not? Why not stop just for a day?"

Shaking her head, Alexandria knew she was being persuaded. They ought to leave. She could give the landlord enough money to ensure Paxten's care. But what if the landlord did not use the funds for a doctor's attendance? Or what if Paxten did not recover rapidly enough to avoid capture by the soldiers who sought him?

Bother the man! The world always became more tangled with him nearby.

She glanced at her niece again, but she had to admit that she wanted to lose this argument. She did not want to leave him—not without knowing he would recover from his injuries.

"We cannot stay too long. I will not jeopardize your safety for his."

Diana smiled. "I doubt you will have to, dear. Now, shall I order us breakfast, and let us do get our things in, for I vow I am sick enough of being in this dress that I could burn it."

"You found a half-naked woman where?" Captain Taliaris stared hard at his lieutenant. Taliaris stood with his hands folded behind his back and his cloak wrapped around him against the dawn chill. Behind him, the eastern sky brightened to pink, but the sun had yet to inch up over the trees and the low roofs of the village cottages. Pale light washed across Lieutenant Paulin's narrow face, giving the man a gaunt, gloomy look.

Taliaris frowned.

They ought to have Marsett by now. Had the man remained in Paris? But where? His rooms had been searched, as had his other known haunts. Which left another answer—Marsett had somehow slipped through the noose set for him.

Taliaris's frown tightened his mouth. He did not like mistakes, least of all those he had made. Mistakes cost lives—and careers. Wars could be lost. But it seemed as if he had miscalculated Marsett's cunning this time. He would not do so again.

Paulin kept himself at rigid attention, as if uncertain of his commander's temper and unwilling to earn himself any rebuke. He took his time with his answer. Taliaris allowed his mouth to relax. He had at least taught his lieutenant to think before acting. Or speaking.

"*Where* is not so important, Captain. But this was." The lieutenant held out a gentleman's blue coat, wrinkled now and stained. "She had it on over her chemise."

Taliaris lifted one eyebrow as he glimpsed the dark-brown

stains on the right side of the coat. Bloodstains. Well, the general's guards had sworn they had hit their target last night.

Taking the coat, Taliaris searched the pockets sewn into the tails. Paulin would have done so as well, but Taliaris repeated the effort, and then tore the silk lining from the coat, just in case something lay hidden. He found nothing. Nothing to show this coat might have been Marsett's.

Paulin hurried on, his voice reedy. "I would have brought her to you to question, sir, but mostly she cries. And I think she gave us already all she knows. She is a maid."

Tossing the coat into the dirt, Taliaris glanced up the road to Paris. In the distance, smoke from the city's chimneys made a faint haze in the pale sky. Mists lay low on the green pastures around the village. Church bells rang nearby, a reminder that it was Sunday.

Taliaris glanced at Paulin. "And the women in the coach?"

"Lady Sandal and her niece. We got that much from her. And her name—Marie-Jeanne Toulon. A man took her dress and left her his coat. She thinks when her mistress discovers this, she will come back for her."

"Did she describe the man?"

"It was dark. She could not see, other than that he frightened her, but when he spoke, he seemed a gentleman—until he made her give up her clothes."

Taliaris's mouth pulled down. "Lucky enough for her that he did not force her into more." Turning away from Paris, Taliaris glanced in the opposite direction.

The narrow lane wound into woods, with deep grooves worn into the mud by passing carriages. How many miles had Marsett managed before the Englishwomen learned that he was not their maid? Ten miles? A hundred? And in what direction? North still? Or had they turned east? Or west?

He wanted to curse his own gallantry. He ought to have sent those Englishwomen back to Paris, but he had thought the ladies a distraction. And—to be ruthlessly truthful—he had allowed a pair of blue eyes to beguile him.

The girl had been lovely beyond words, with the torchlight playing over that soft, round face. With those golden curls, and those huge, luminous eyes. And the vibrant flash of spirit that had caught him.

Another mistake.

Well, it would seem that he would meet up with the little beauty again. For her sake, he would hope to meet her soon. Marsett could be a danger to her—as he had proven to the general's wife. And it seemed from the maid's description that this Marsett could make himself charming before he revealed himself as the low cur he was.

Turning to Paulin, Taliaris snapped out his orders. "Leave three men here with the maid. They are to keep her under guard. The rest are to be ready to ride in a quarter hour."

Paulin nodded. "Yes, sir."

"Pick your men well for the ones who are to stay—I don't want to learn they decided to drink up whatever is to be found. And make certain the fastest horse is left with them."

"Fastest?"

"Yes, Lieutenant. If someone does come for this Marie-Jeanne, I want a rider to bring me word of it. For I want these Englishwomen—and that damn Marsett—found. Today!"

Fever dreams—they had to be fever dreams. Restless, hot, he turned, trying to wake from them. Alexandria stood over him, laughing, holding a smoking pistol in her hand. He glanced down to see the black-edged hole in his skin—and he clawed at it, trying to pull it out of him.

"You don't have heart enough to bleed."

He glanced up at the mocking words to see Lisette D'Aeth now holding the gun and smiling. "Andria? Where's Andria?" he muttered, twisting again, desperate to find her.

Something cool smoothed his forehead. He turned into it. Then the world shifted.

He stood outside a London town house. He knew it at once.

A perfect jewel of a place, tucked into a park on the edges of Mayfair. A small house, only two floors, square but of perfect proportion. Iron fences marked the property. Torches burned beside the front steps, giving an orange hue to the white columns. The upper windows blazed with light—Lady Sandal and her lord entertained tonight.

He hated the place. But he had not been able to stay away, even though he knew she was married. Even though he knew he was dragging them both into scandal.

He waited now as he had ten years before, standing on the cobblestone street outside the gates. Only something was not right. What was different? Ah, yes. The rain. It had been cold that night. Cold and wet as only England could be in February. A miserable night. The coach driver huddled under his sodden coat, and the pair of horses attached to the hired carriage stood with their heads down and tails clamped tight.

Only he did not feel the rain—how could he, hot as he was. He pulled at his clothes, wanting to drag them off. Someone murmured something and a hand smoothed his face. But he was still waiting. Waiting in the rain. Waiting.

And then he saw the door to the Sandal house open and the figure step out.

No! Not again. He did not want to live this again.

He turned away, opened the carriage, and saw Alexandria inside—as she had not been that night. That night she had betrayed him. She looked as she had then; dressed in white silk, silver spangles glinting on her gown, diamonds around her neck and pinned in her hair, her skin so pale under the hair piled into curls on her head. She leaned forward from the coach, stretching out an arm gloved in white kid to the elbow.

He smiled at her but then glanced back to the house, puzzled. So who had stepped from the house? Sandal?

But no. Moonlight shone on gold braid. Medals flashed. A uniform? He recognized the silver military whiskers as General D'Aeth raised a dueling pistol and pointed the wicked, long barrel at Alexandria.

With a smothered shout, eyes snapping wide, his heart pounding, Paxten woke. He tried to sit up, managed to lift his head, and that exhausted him. The world spun, so he closed his eyes and fell back against a feather pillow that smelled faintly musty.

Silk rustled. He reached out toward the sound, and his fingers closed over a slim wrist. "Andria?"

"Hush—my aunt is resting in the chair by the fire. You have had us worried, Mr. Marsett."

Prying open his eyes, he glanced up into the face of a golden-haired beauty. Blue eyes, a rounded, stubborn chin, and soft cheeks. Frowning, he stared at her. Who was she? Then memories drifted back—fleeing Paris, the maid, the carriage ride, and they had reached an inn, had they not?

Shutting his eyes, he muttered, "The niece with the edge to her pretty cots. Dovecotes. A sweet dove. Where's Andria?"

"You are babbling. But the doctor said we should expect as much. Your fever got dreadfully high. Here, can you drink this? It is nearly dawn, but you and my aunt would both be better for a few hours more sleep."

An arm slid under his head and a glass pressed to his lips. Liquid, cool and faintly bitter, slipped into his mouth. He drank it, greedy for anything wet. He managed two swallows, then pushed her hand and the glass away.

"What is it?" he asked, and he heard the slurring in his words.

"An opiate and something else—broth of some sort. Chicken or oxtail."

He made a face. "A tail to tell. Throw it out and bring me water—or tea. Strong tea. I dislike the dreams that gives me."

Cool fingers touched his face again. Twisting his head, he opened his eyes and stared at her. She smiled—Mother Mary, what a beauty. Far more so than her aunt. But that smile brought out a family resemblance. The girl's mouth was not as wide, but something about how the brows arched, and how the expression lit her face from within, reminded him of Andria.

Or of how she had once been. Could she still smile like that, with such innocence and life?

His glance slid to the fireside, then his mouth twisted.

Alexandria had fallen asleep in an enormous wing chair, its brocade upholstery worn into shades of brown. Her long legs stretched out to the dying embers in the fireplace, and her skirts had ridden up so that he could see a pair of trim ankles. She had always had lovely ankles, slim and set off by calves made shapely by her love of walking. They had once walked miles together. Her head had tipped to the side, and her wrist dangled over the chair arm, loose with sleep.

Something tightened in his chest.

Closing his eyes, he turned away. "She still snores."

"I beg your pardon! My aunt is too refined for that. She is—well, that is merely the deep breathing of one fast asleep. And she has earned her rest. She was up most of the night with you—you are not a good patient, you know. Twice we had to call in the landlord to keep you in bed. You were raving."

Lead weights now hung from his eyelids, but he pulled open his eyes to stare at the girl. "I was? About what?"

"Just nonsense." Relieved, he closed his eyes again. Then she added, "You did go on and on about a Lisette. Who is she?"

"Ah, *ma petite fille*, the opiate must be clouding my mind—did you ask something?"

"I did. And if you do not answer, I suppose I can have my aunt ask you tomorrow."

His mouth twisted. "A threat, *ma fille?* Never wise—it makes you no friends and tells an enemy your plan."

"We are not enemies, I hope. And that was not a threat—a threat would be to say that I shall give you some of the other noxious concoction the doctor left for you, which smells vile, and is made with watered wine and a raw egg."

She spoke with such loathing that Paxten gave a dry chuckle, then winced at the dull stab of pain along his side. He heard a scrape of a chair on the wooden floor and more rustling fabric.

And then she said, her voice deliciously low and soft, "Well, if you will not tell me about Lisette, then why do you not tell me how is it that you know my aunt so well?"

Six

He did not answer, but Diana knew he had heard, for one side of his mouth lifted in a rather cynical smile. She had almost asked if he and her aunt had been lovers, and now she was glad she had not. Bad enough to have that mocking smile. It would have been unbearable to have him laughing at her for asking prying questions, as if she knew nothing of the world or how to judge the level of intimacy between a man and a woman.

Twisted smile or not, he was shamefully handsome—in a rough sort of way, with dark stubble shaping a strong jaw, and him lying there, chest naked above the fresh bandages and well-muscled arms bare above the counterpane. An intriguing scar angled across his left shoulder in a short, jagged mark. A dueling scar, perhaps? Or had he been a highwayman? Or something equally dashing? She could see him as such. And she could see how her aunt might be attracted to him.

But had they been lovers?

Something certainly lay between them. Only a child would be unaware of the tension that crackled.

However, she had little time now to ask about it. His regaining his senses gave her the opportunity, but with him conscious again she doubted she would be allowed into his room. Certainly not without a maid, or her aunt, as a chaperone.

To judge by the look of him, she was not entirely certain she cared to be in his rooms with him fully awake and no one else nearby. That rough quality to him—the scar, the hard muscles, and even the fact that he had thought to hide in their carriage—quite fascinated but left her wary. All considered, he could not really be very much of a gentleman.

He even seemed intent on ignoring her, so she asked, impatient with him, "You are not going to answer me, are you?"

The opiate she had given him thickened his voice into an even deeper rumble. "Answer what—nonsense with nonsense? How is it anything happens? The wrong turn taken, the wrong place arrived at. Perhaps it is just that fate is not done with me any more than I am done with your aunt."

His eyes opened to narrow slits—dark eyes framed by hard lines. Then he yawned. Thick lashes drifted closed and his face relaxed, easing the lines and giving him a deceptive innocence.

Frowning, Diana folded her arms. She did not like how he had spoken just then—not done with her aunt, was he? Sitting back in her chair, she glanced at her aunt and then back to the sleeping man again. Was he to be trusted? She doubted it. Which meant she must have his secrets out.

She twisted her mouth, then muttered, "If you are going to be good for my aunt, that is one thing, but if you are not. . . ." Leaning forward, she hoped that even in his sleep he might hear her. "If you are not, I shall make very certain you regret it!"

For the second time in two days, Alexandria woke with a stiff neck and an aching body. She dragged her eyes open, took in the cold black grate of the fireplace, with its charred bits of wood, and rubbed her arms against the chill in the room. Straightening, she stretched. Muscles pulled in her back and something popped in her neck. She had fallen asleep in a chair—and left the bed she had paid for unused. What waste! Putting a hand to her curls, she dragged her fingers through tangles. Then she rose, smoothed her gown, and went to Paxten's bedside.

At the sight of him, tension eased from her shoulders.

His chest rose and fell with even breaths, and his skin held a hint of normal color—not that hectic flush of last night. She touched the back of her fingers to his forehead. Only slightly warm.

Voice soft, she murmured, "You wretch—how very like you to give me palpitations."

He said nothing in reply. Still sleeping, thank heavens. She ought to go to her room and tidy herself. But still she watched him. The doctor had bled him last night, and had left something to help him sleep and something else for him to take today when he woke. The man, elderly and jovial, had seemed to think the wound—a deep red gash across Paxten's ribs—would heal well enough. The ribs had been bruised but not broken.

Last night, when Diana had translated what the doctor had said, Alexandria had been relieved. But then the fever set in. She nearly sent for the doctor again. However, he had already warned them to expect a bad night.

The sound of horses now in the yard below drew her attention, and she hurried to the window, her brow tight with worry. She relaxed when she saw only a farmer and his wagon outside, apparently there to sell produce to the landlord. No soldiers. Nothing to alarm. No one had found them.

But how long until someone did come after Paxten? She would be foolish not to assume the worst—whoever hunted Paxten would eventually figure out that he had escaped in her coach. Which meant they would soon be searching for her carriage.

Turning away from the window, she went back to Paxten's side. She smoothed the blanket over him. She had promised Diana a day—and that had been spent already. She could not afford to waste more time. She knew exactly what needed to be done to keep Diana safe. Which meant that she must act.

Quietly, she let herself out of Paxten's room. She would need to speak to Diana after she had washed her face and seen to her own needs. Then there was the carriage to order, and the trunks to see to. So much to do. But at least she would not be leaving Paxten at death's door.

The hard crack of a carriage whip jolted Paxten from his nightmares and had him bolting upright in bed, clutching his side before he actually identified that the sound was not the shot fired in his dreams. He glanced around, aware of the narrow bed under him, of sheets tangled around his naked legs. And of the pressure of something around his throbbing ribs. He glanced down at the white bandages around his middle, and then rubbed a hand across his face. A day of stubble scrubbed his fingertips.

The memories trickled into place. The doctor. The medicines poured down him. Ah, yes. But had he dreamed of talking to Alexandria's niece last night, or had that really happened? He certainly had dreamed of Alexandria. And of too many other things from his past.

Outside in the yard, a carriage harness jingled. Curious, he rose, padding across the bare wood. He reached the window in time to see Alexandria's coach—fresh horses attached, the coachman up front, and the footman standing at the back—as it rounded the bend in the road that led away from the village.

He pressed one palm against the window.

She had gone. Left him. An ache tightened in his chest. He shook his head. What a smart woman she had become—so very good at looking after herself. But then, she had always been sensible about these things. And utterly capable of parting company with him—any number of times, it seemed.

He forced a crooked smile. Ah, but what did it matter? So this ended his plans. That was all. If she had gone, she'd gone. It left him . . . irritated, that was all. Yes, annoyed that she had outfoxed his schemes. Well, so it went. He would encourage the touch of relief that she had taken away the temptation to do his worst with her.

With a hand pressed to his sore side, he made his way back

to the bed. Rising fast had left him light-headed, and he was glad enough to lie down. Had she left money for his room, or was he on his own there? No matter. He had survived worse. That winter in Russia for one. Their parting a decade ago for another.

Closing his eyes, he decided to worry about all of it later.

Then the door creaked open and clicked closed, a bustle of skirts came closer, and the pungent aroma of hot tea washed over him. So she had left someone to look after him—a comely tavern maid, he would hope.

He opened his eyes to see not the maid he expected, but Alexandria, putting a wooden tray on the seat of a chair that stood next to the bed.

He stared at her. It could not be fever dreams still. Could it? His eyebrows snapped tight along with his temper. "If you are here, then where's your coach gone?"

She offered a calm smile. "To Calais. Do you still take milk in your tea? I managed that, but no sugar." She poured dark tea into a pottery mug and served him as if using fine porcelain, not mismatched bits of china.

Easing himself up on one elbow, he took the mug and sipped. Then he realized his thirst and drank it back, the liquid going down warm and easy. It lacked only a splash of brandy.

"More?" she offered. "It took forever to teach the landlord's wife how to make a decent pot. She simply did not understand that one must leave the water on long enough to boil properly."

He smiled at her as she filled his mug again and added milk from a small, chipped pitcher. "I suppose I should not say this, but I thought you had abandoned me to my fate. What did you do—send your niece on without you?"

She glanced at him, those elegant, light brown eyebrows arching with surprise. At what he wondered? That he would confide the truth to her, or that he would think she might part company with her charge? "I sent my coach on with the landlord's cousin and her two daughters—and you may repay me for the amount it took to bribe them to make the trip. Are you hungry? The doctor left word that you might eat gruel today."

He made a face. "Spare me. But you may have a beefsteak sent up."

"I think not. The goal is to have you able to travel soon and not down with fever again. Gruel and tea today. Tomorrow you—"

"Tomorrow I shall be up and ordering my own meals, and will be well able to travel. As to repayment—*ma chère,* my pockets are to let, though that may change if my luck shifts and if you care to stake me some coins. But how are we to go anywhere now that you've stranded us? What were you thinking, Andria?"

She had poured herself a mug of tea, and now she sipped from it and studied him over its rim. Amazing how little she had changed—a few lines more around those wide gray eyes, and a less-slender figure. But he had once thought her too thin—unhappily thin. How very long ago that seemed.

"I was thinking," she said, "that the doctor said at least three days of rest or you may risk an infection. And if whoever is after you thinks you might be in my carriage, why not send it along and give them something to chase. My brother will not be happy that I have lost his coach. But I suspect I should not have been able to get it across the Channel anyway, and I kept most of our luggage. And some of Gaston's clothes—he was one of my footmen, and while his clothes will be too large for you, they look more respectable than your own."

He raised his mug of tea to her. "I am impressed."

"Please do not be. Expertise in deception is nothing admirable. However, since you have involved me—and my niece—in your troubles, I should like to know exactly whom we are attempting to avoid. Those soldiers did not seem interested in you as just another Englishman to arrest."

Paxten sipped his tea and began to sift through what lies he might tell, but Alexandria surprised him again by stating bluntly, "Spare yourself the trouble of any inventions. I have already guessed this involves a Madame Lisette. And, no, I have not become a mind reader. You muttered the name last night when the fever had you."

"I suppose that's only fair."

"What do you mean by that?"

He only smiled for an answer.

Her lips tightened, then she said, "I assume she is your paramour. And married to a jealous man?"

"How quick you are to think the worst of me."

"And how right am I?"

Unrepentant, he lifted one shoulder—the good one—but he still winced at the effort. "Near enough to the mark. Though from the starch in your voice it sounds as if you thought I would become a monk after you sent me away." Color bled into her cheeks. He grinned. "Ah, you did think it—you imagined me pining for you."

She drew herself up, but he kept grinning, for he had spent far too long doing just that, dragging himself around the world and finding every other woman lacking when compared with her. He would be properly boiled himself before he admitted to her just how long it had taken to forever harden his heart.

Those eyebrows arched over her gray eyes again. "I thought you not such a rogue as to take up with married women."

"Why not? I took up with you."

The color flamed in her cheeks, two bright splashes of hot pink against the soft cream of her skin. He thought for a moment that she might dash her mug of tea into his face. Then she swallowed hard and gave a small nod. "Yes, you did. But you did not learn then that such liaisons only lead to grief?"

"Oh, with Lisette it was leading to something quite pleasurable."

"You have an odd notion of pleasure if such leads you to nearly being shot to death."

He decided on blunt truth. To shock her. And to serve fair warning that what lay between them was far from finished. "That I did not plan. Actually, I displeased the lady—I called her by your name."

She stared at him, suspicion in her eyes. He met her gaze with one as open as he could make it. "I do not believe you," she said.

"As you like. She certainly was not amused. She began screaming rape, and then I found out about the wisdom in not bedding a general's wife."

Alexandria's eyebrows snapped together, and he expected her to blister him now with righteous disapproval. Instead, she said, her tone indignant, "Rape? You? Honestly, what a ridiculous charge? As if you ever had the need for such a thing, when you had but to smile at any woman to have her melting at your feet!"

Amused, he sipped his tea. Still the innocent, despite everything. To think that a woman's availability and interest had much to do with some men's appetites. But she was right in one thing. The dark violence of rape had never stirred him. He preferred to court a woman's surrender, to coax it from her, to steal it with kisses and soft touches. As he intended to do with her.

But telling her that much truth would spoil his plans.

So he only sipped his tea, then said, "I did not feel inclined to defend myself to General D'Aeth." Her eyes widened and he asked, "Ah, so you know the general?"

She nodded. "And his wife—she is, well, I should call her a flirt."

"I should call her a *racoleuse*—and, no, I will not translate that for you."

"I have not asked, now, have I? But I can guess it is as far from polite as you are. I do wish, however, that you would have thought twice before taking my maid's place. You are a good deal of bother, you know."

Reaching out, he gave her his mug, but after she took it

from him, he gripped her wrist. "Yes, I know. So you must allow me to make it up to you."

She stiffened. "Please, do not."

His thumb brushed her skin. *"Qu'est-ce que c'est?"*

"You know very well what it is. And I know at least that in French."

"Ah, but I only meant that I could repay you in that I could see to obtaining transportation for us. What did you think I meant?"

"I know what you meant, and it is not that. Do not make me regret my decision to help you."

"But we have so many regrets between us already. What are a few more?"

"You are going to force me to pour the rest of the tea in this pot over your head!"

He grinned. "You may try—but if you think I will allow that, you mistake me for that doddering old fool you married."

"Bertram was not that old."

"You don't, I see, defend his doddering. But I do misspeak. He was not as great a fool as I. Why did you not leave me here, *ma chère?* Why stay? Are you still making choices from what you think is your duty?"

The color rose in her cheeks, but she met his gaze, her own assured, even though he could see her chest rise and fall with rapid, short breaths. "Is that all you think you are to me? A case of Christian charity? That I have no feelings here? That what we . . . what we once meant to each other does not matter to me?"

His hand tightened around her wrist. "It did not seem to matter to you when last we parted."

She shook her head. "You always judged my feelings by how well I capitulated to your own, and I failed you there. However, I do still have some care for you, even though you have obviously not changed one bit!"

"Oh, I've changed. How could I not?"

One skeptical eyebrow lifted. She glanced down at the

hand he still held. She had not tried to pull away. A perverse desire swept into him to tug, to drag her onto the bed with him and have her, whether she willed it or not. To let out the violence in him.

And he had just thought himself beyond such tastes.

But perhaps he was. For he could not do it. She had put him in her debt by staying. And he wanted more than her body—he wanted her heart, vulnerable, open, ready to be cut out. He wanted to know she could—and would—feel anguish.

For that he needed time.

Letting go of her, he lay back on the bed. He slipped a smile in place. "I am a demon to torment you when you bring me tea. Of course, I might be better behaved if you brought me something to eat—you can satisfy at least one of my hungers."

With a swish of skirts, she strode to the door. There she paused. "When were you ever satisfied with anything, Paxten? I shall have your beefsteak sent up to you."

She slammed out of the room. He stared at the door a moment, then chuckled. The Alexandria he had once known would never have slammed a door. No, she had always been too afraid of giving offense. Of not doing the right thing. It seemed he was not the only one to have changed.

But had she stayed with him out of that damned chain of responsibility that had once bound her? Because of the memory of affection? No—he could not believe that. She had stood still in his hold, her face indifferent, but the pulse had quickened in her wrist. She still loved to lie to him.

And he was indeed a demon to torment her. He smiled again, but without any humor, for he had just begun. With her, he would prove himself an utter devil. But first he would have to earn her trust. And that meant starting to act like the gentleman he had never been.

* * *

As soon as she was out of the room, Alexandria leaned against the door, fury racing through her. Not fury at him, but at herself. She wished she had some impolite words in French that she could mutter to vent her feeling. Instead, she had only the proper English taught to her.

Oh, curse it all!

A quarter hour with him and she was explaining herself, wanting something from him that he could not give, and back to defending poor Bertram.

Poor, poor Bertram. He ought never to have married. But she had realized that only in the year after Jules had been born, when it had become apparent that Bertram considered his duty done to get an heir, and that there would be no more children. Nor any attempts in bedding her to get them.

Poor Bertram, indeed. He would have made a wonderful bachelor uncle—always pleasant, ever the correct gentleman, ready to offer light flirtation and capable of doing not much more than that with any woman. He had not done so well as a husband. Perhaps she ought to have paid more heed when her mother told her—after Bertram had asked her parents for her hand—that he would never give her a moment's concern. He had not. He never took a mistress. Never glanced at other women. Never stayed late at his club. Never did anything that might upset the routine of his life.

How had he actually managed to get her with child, and to produce a son? He had done so little else in his life.

But that sounded unkind, and she had never wanted to be unkind to him. He tried to be decent in his own way. He never raised his voice or hand to anyone. Never drank too much. Never gambled away his fortune. And he had no need for companionship or affection other than from his male friends.

He had also been shocked down to the soles of his perfectly fit boots when she had asked for a divorce.

"Chetwynds don't divorce," he had said, sounding as horrified as if she had suggested they both walk naked down St. James's Street. Those, however, had not been the words that had finally turned her away from her plan to run away with Paxten.

Why had she learned too late that the sort of man who did give a woman concerns was the sort who lifted her pulse? Paxten's sort. Hot-tempered, hot-blooded, a man who admired every woman who crossed his path, who created trouble around him and then laughed at it. He had been the opposite of staid Bertram. And he had come into her life just when she needed that maddening, passionate disorder to fill the emptiness of a barren marriage. She had almost thrown away everything for him.

If only she had not . . .

That will do. You promised yourself no regrets.

Still, she had them. Paxten had been right about that.

Straightening, she pushed her feelings back into place. She would not indulge them. Not after so many years of strict discipline to hold herself together. But her son no longer needed a capable mother. And she no longer had the ties of her husband and his family. She had only . . . what? Dutiful choices?

Bother Paxten for always knowing her better than she did herself!

She could admit it now that he had forced her to look. She had told herself that she stayed from a sense of concern for him. She had felt so virtuous to be sending her carriage away, sacrificing for another. She had convinced herself that she owed him such an obligation. But now she saw that hidden excitement, the shimmer of hope that there might be more between herself and Paxten again.

Paxten had stripped away the pretense between them. She saw the truth in herself now. And he had also shown her that while physical sparks might remain, so did deep scars that still hurt if touched.

With a shake of her head, she started down the stairs. At the foot, she paused and glanced back. If she had any real courage, she would stride back up, go into his room, pin him to his bed, and kiss him until she knew for a certainty that whatever lay between them was but a physical attraction that could be mastered.

But what if that was a lie?

Skin warm, she bit her lower lip.

This seemed a dangerous, one-sided game. Paxten might know her better than she did herself, but what did she really know of the man he had become? Oh, yes, he could attract with that sensual charm of his, but she had also seen the calculation in his eyes. A dark edge ran through him, one that had not been there before. And now she had stranded herself with him.

Oh, but perhaps, perhaps, she was just being overly sensitive about all this. They had been shocked to see each other last night; and they were both fatigued. Yet, perhaps that was what kept them on edge. She could not tell—and that alone ought to warn her to keep her distance.

However, they had once meant so much to each other. And she found she could not let go of that. She did not want to. With Bertram in his grave and Jules grown, the only thing that stood between them really was the shadow of their past. Such an insubstantial thing. Such an uncertain thing.

So why did it seem so insurmountably large?

Paxten's good intentions to mind his manners lasted until the gruel arrived instead of his beef. A thin slip of a maid with dark hair and sallow skin brought it to him, along with Alexandria's niece, who bustled about, opening windows, rattling on in schoolgirl French, and pausing only to arrange in a white vase the spring wildflowers she had picked. The girl's chatter amused him. Then he glanced at the watery gruel in the bowl on the tray.

He looked at the maid, then picked up the bowl and threw it. He had good aim, and the startled squawk of chickens came in through the window that the bowl had gone out. He wished them *bon appétit* with any remains they could find.

Then he said, "I asked for beef."

Wide-eyed, the maid started to hurry out to fetch what he wanted, but Alexandria's niece stopped her. "Please forgive my uncle, and bring him more gruel. Aunt's orders, dear Uncle," she added, showing small white teeth in something that might be meant as a smile.

He lifted one eyebrow. "She told me she would send me the beefsteak I wanted."

"Well, that is not what she—what are you doing? Stop that! You are not supposed to be out of bed!"

He paused with his bare feet swung out and onto the floor and the bedcovers the only thing between his skin and the world. "Am I not? But if no one will bring me food I can eat, then I must fetch my own."

"But . . . but you are not decent."

He flashed a grin. "I've not been that for years. But if you mean I have no clothes, then either bring me breeches and a shirt or close your eyes. Or bring me real food."

With a good imitation of her aunt, her chin lifted and she folded her arms. "You are bluffing."

He winked at the maid, and then said to the niece, "Hungry men do not bluff, my little one." Pushing up off the bed, he started to stand. The girl's blue eyes widened. The maid stared, her mouth hanging open.

Before he could gain his feet, the girl gave a squeak, then hurried out the door, dragging the maid with her even though the maid stared back over her shoulder at him, admiration warming her eyes. As he stood, he heard their rapid footsteps hurrying away. Would they return with food? Or with Alexandria?

In either case, he was bored with lying in bed. The landlord had come up earlier to shave him, but now his stomach grumbled its complaints of neglect.

He dragged a sheet around him, clutching the ends of it at one hip. Not the most fashionable garb. But good enough. He had to wait a moment for the room to steady, then he started for the door, intent on finding something to eat and to wear, and wishing this dizziness would go away.

The hallway also kept wanting to tilt on its side, so he paused in the doorway to lean on it and catch his breath. When he heard the firm step on the stairs, he stayed where he was, waiting for her.

A moment later, Alexandria came up the narrow stairway, her skirts lifted, showing those trim ankles of hers. She had changed, he saw, into a different gown from this morning—something very pretty, he thought, in a deep gold with a pattern in it of red and brown. She had tucked a white scarf around the low neckline, and a garnet-and-topaz brooch pinned the scarf between her lovely high breasts.

He watched her for a moment, eyes narrowed, then made her an elegant bow, baring one leg from the sheet to do so. Then he asked, "I thought you were going to send me up some beef?"

She shook her head. "You are as pale as that linen you are wearing. Please go back to bed."

"Only if you come with me."

Eyebrows arching, she came forward and wrapped her arm around him. Then she looked up at him, gray eyes almost silver in the light. "Very well. I shall."

Seven

Her agreement surprised him. "You shall? What is this—more false promises? Such as my meat."

"Are you still harping on that? I was annoyed when I said I should give you what is bad for you. But what if we compromise—on beef broth?"

He laughed. Then he winced, and moved his arm from the doorjamb to lay it over her shoulders. She had been speaking mostly French, but with English words used whenever she could not find a translation. She mangled the language, but he found it charming. It made her seem less the so-very-correct Lady Sandal.

He slanted her a glance. "Is that what you want in my bed too—compromise?"

"What I want in your bed is you!" She spoke quick and sharp, and then seemed to realize what she had said, for the flush streamed up from her neck and into her face.

He spoke quickly, and in English, intending the words for her alone. "You could have me there—just by asking. Will you ask now, *ma chère?*"

The images flooded his mind, sending his senses reeling. Her naked and arching with pleasure. Silken hair loose. His hands on that creamy skin of hers. He had reason once to call her Lady Scandal. Reason to know she could be as wanton as any Parisian *amazone*. And he wanted to see her like that again. Wanted to see her eyes glazed by passion. Wanted to hear soft, helpless moans of shivering pleasure from her. Wanted her lost to everything but him.

His hand stroked down from that slender neck, over a supple back, and to a waist almost as trim as he remembered. With that memory, his body stirred. The sheet slipped from his loosened fingers, shifting dangerously low. He ignored it and brushed his lips against her cheek. "Ah, but it's been so long, too long, since I touched you. I could hold you like this forever."

"That is an absurd thing to say," she answered, her tone clipped but with a betraying quiver underneath.

"Then I am absurd. Or still hot with fever, and not with the intoxication of you."

Trying to focus on her task—and not on his lips, nor the caress of his hand, which inched lower on her back—Alexandria took hold of the ends of the sheet with one hand. She kept her other arm around him. She tried to be careful of his wound, and so she ended with her hand pressed against his bare skin just below the bandages and above his narrow hips. Her throat tightened. It had been too long. But he was in no condition for this. Neither was she, with too little sleep and too many things happening too fast.

She must remember, too, that he had been shot not that long ago for being in another woman's bed. But why did that not seem to matter so much with his lips brushing across her jaw?

"What of your desire for beef?" she said, focusing on the practical and pulling him toward his bed.

His voice dropped lower. "Why must I choose? Why can I not have both?"

"I ought to call the landlord to assist you."

"But you are so much more charming. And I think perhaps you smell better too." He pressed his nose to her neck and then rubbed his lips from her neck to her cheek. "You smell of . . . of onions actually. What have you been eating?"

"Onion soup—the landlord's wife is an excellent cook."

He pulled back from her, his eyes bright with indignation. "You eat such things and send me gruel—you torture me!"

"No, that would be allowing you to make yourself deathly ill!" With the words, she pulled away from him and then pushed hard on his chest. The bed caught him on the back of his knees, and he tumbled back, arms flung out as he lost his balance. He ended up lying diagonally across the narrow bed. Bending over, she lifted his feet and put them up on the bed.

The sheet had twisted around him, revealing one muscular thigh and a glimpse of flat, hard hip and stomach. She tried not to stare at the bare skin, the taut muscles—how unfair that ten years sat so well on a man. And how lovely.

The momentary distraction gave him time. Grabbing her hand, he gave a sharp tug and pulled her down so that she lay next to him, pressed against his uninjured side. He smiled at her. "Now are you happy? I am in bed again."

"Paxten! This is not good for you!"

"Let me judge that," he said, nuzzling her neck.

She pushed against him, but he had his arm around her and more strength than she expected. Parting her lips, she started to reason with him.

He stole her words, covering her mouth with his.

Heat rushed into her in a dizzying, sweet flush. His tongue brushed across her lips, and she let out a breath. Oh, she had forgotten the drugging passion of him, how soft his lips could be, how demanding, how caressing.

She wound her arm around his neck and arched against him. His palm brushed across her breast and then his fingers closed there, pulling another sigh of pleasure from her. She pushed against his chest but without any real desire to free herself. Ah, it had been too long. So very, very long.

But then his kiss deepened to something harsh, something more demanding, and panic flared inside her.

The clatter of hooves, and the shouts from the yard, gave her reason enough to at last drag herself from his grip.

Dazed, she rose from the bed. He stared at her, eyes

narrowed and an angry flare in them, but then he seemed to hear the commotion from below. His eyebrows lifted as he glanced toward the open window.

Alexandria moved to the window, heart thudding hard and her stomach quivering—from Paxten, or the alarming sounds coming from the stable yard? She did not stop to find an answer. Instead, she brushed at her hair and looked out.

At the sight of the uniforms, she spun around and the word came out with a panicked breath, "Soldiers!"

Paxten muttered something in French, then pushed up from the bed, sheets tangled around his legs. "Where are my breeches? Do you know, does this inn have a back entrance?"

Frustration simmered in Taliaris. Having to stop at every village for word of three women traveling in a coach made for slow work. But he wanted no more mistakes. The trail had been here and then gone, but always it led toward Calais. He still could not believe it. Did these English have no sense to take side roads? To vary their direction? Or were they so arrogant, they did not fear anyone would follow? Or perhaps he was on the wrong trail entirely, following innocents who did not need to hide?

That last worry made him cautious. And so he took his time, stopping at every town, every village, every farmhouse near a crossroad, accounting for every change of horse they made and every glimpse of that black coach.

They'd had one piece of luck—a footman had indeed come back for Marie-Jeanne. Now they would see if he had told them the truth when they had questioned him.

Swinging off his horse, Taliaris handed the reins to his orderly and watched as his lieutenant barked orders to dismount. Then he glanced around this sorry excuse for a village. The English had at last left the main road to come here. The footman had not wanted to say anything—a loyalty Taliaris could admire even if it was misplaced. But putting a man in front of a firing squad made most forget noble ideals in place of survival. Before muskets could even be shouldered, the footman had betrayed the name and direction of this village as the place where the English had stopped.

But it had taken long enough, first to ride back to interrogate the footman, and then longer still to ride here. Would the English still be here? Well, even if they weren't, his men needed food now, and their mounts needed water and rest. They would stop. And he would hope their quarry had been foolish enough to feel safe and remain.

The landlord came out from his inn, a frown in place as he took in the soldiers and horses in his yard. Taliaris gave the man the same examination. Not every Frenchman held as deep an affection for the First Consul as did those who served him in the army. Some called Bonaparte the Little Corsican, never mind that Corsica had been part of France for years now. Others called him dictator, and murderer of the Revolution. And a few still proclaimed the Bourbons as the true rulers of France. Of course, they did not do so in public. But Taliaris had heard the whispers.

And this landlord did not look pleased to see them.

Wiping his hands on his apron, Gustave Lepic singled out the man who seemed in command. Not the one shouting orders, but the one who stood watching everyone else jump. Armies—bah! Bad for business. Too often they ate and drank, and when the time came for the bill, they said it ought to be a glory to serve those who served France and left without paying. But he kept those thoughts to himself and gave them a stupid grin.

In troubled times, a fool might stay alive. And these times seemed always troubled.

"Good day, General. And what may I do for such fine soldiers of France? Is it food you need? Drink? My brother owns the best vineyard in Champagne."

No jovial smile answered him, just a face that could have been carved of oak. He had to look up at the man—a tall fellow. His shako made him seem even taller. The dolman jacket swung over one shoulder by a cord, and the gold braid across his chest also made him dauntingly broad. But he had a young man's face. An earnest face. Deadly so.

Gustave kept smiling. What else did one do with men who carried muskets and sabers and had the right to do anything in the name of France and the man who had made himself Her master?

"We are looking for some English. Two women with their maid. They would be traveling by coach. They also might have lost the maid in place of a man—an injured man."

English—ah, he had known it. The girl had that look to her with that fair skin and golden hair, and the lady, well, no Frenchwoman spoke so little as she.

Rubbing his chin, Gustave took time to answer. Was there a profit to be made here? Not from these men but from how grateful an Englishwoman might be that she had been kept safe? Finally, he said, "Well, now, a coach left just this morning, it did. With three women inside. They hired fresh horses from me."

"Describe them."

Gustave hesitated. So far he had not lied—he had said nothing that could come back to him in accusations. What could he say now without stretching his neck out?

His hesitation did not serve. This time, as he rubbed his jaw and tried to look befuddled, the soldier's mouth thinned with impatience. Then he turned and called out, "Search the inn!"

Gustave pulled in a breath. If they found those guests of his, what would they do to him? Might they take him for something other than a fat fool and arrest him as well?

He hurried to the doorway, his apron flapping, the sweat cold on his forehead. "Ah, but, sirs, I run a good, decent place. Boots stomping through my inn will disturb my guests and frighten my maid. Come, why do you not allow me to show you to a snug parlor instead, where you may have some bread and cheese, and good wine to wash it down?"

The soldiers glanced at him, then pushed past, shoving him aside. He might as well have been talking to a storm, telling it not to blow. The man who had ordered the search remained in the stable yard, one hand resting on his saber.

Temper lost, Gustave swung on him. "It is not enough you take our sons and our crops, but now you have to take our homes apart! War! Always it is war with this Bonaparte! Why can you not—"

"Careful, innkeep! You do not want to say things you will have to repeat before the Minister of Justice."

Sagging, Gustave slunk back.

And then a shout came from the inn, from upstairs. "Captain—in here!"

Face pale, sweat stinging as it dripped into his eyes, Gustave watched the captain stride into the inn, his saber rattling at his side. He hurried after, his heart beating so hard it made him ill.

Could he pretend outrage to learn his guests were not French, that they had deceived him—and they had. Of course, he had not asked too closely about them once he saw their gold. *Mary, Mother of God, help me now.* His stomach quivered, but he resisted the urge to cross himself. However, he did put a hand up to rub his throat, for he could already feel the noose tighten.

The captain took the stairs three at a time. Gustave rushed after him, and then stopped in the doorway and stared into a room empty of anything other than its usual furniture, too many soldiers, and three heavy, open portmanteaus.

One man held up a pink silk dress. "Someone left in a hurry, sir. Quick enough to leave these."

Gustave blinked. The English were gone?

Gold braid loomed before him and he looked up into a tight-set face. He swallowed his fear, but it lodged in his throat.

"Tell me again about those women who left this morning in their carriage—and tell me this time why they left their dresses behind."

* * *

Alexandria sat with her jewel box at her feet, Diana pressed against her on the left and Paxten on the right. They sat three to a bench seat designed to hold two, and she knew Paxten's every movement. She felt him turn to glance behind them, knew when he braced his leg against the gig to better handle a turn, and knew also when his shoulders sagged with the effort his exertions cost him. But he would not allow her to take the reins even though she had offered three times now.

The worry had to come out somehow, so she put it into simmering indignation. "That brooch cost eighty pounds!"

He glanced at her, then looked back to the road. He had kept the pair of horses harnessed to the gig at a brisk trot ever since they had left the farmhouse that lay at the edge of the village. Judging from the sun's position, they traveled west, but Alexandria would not have made a wager on that. At least the sun shone, the air held a touch of spring warmth, and the road stretched open before them.

A smile curved his mouth, even though she could glimpse white brackets of pain there as well. "You ought to appreciate, then, that you travel in a most expensive carriage."

"Did you have to pay that farmer with that particular brooch?" she asked.

His answer came back unruffled, as amused as ever. "It was not a time for bargaining, as I recall, and it caught his eye. Was it an heirloom?"

"I would never have allowed you to give away any of the Chetwynd family jewels!" *And now I sound like my mother— or worse, like Bertram's mother,* she decided. Was she becoming that—a stiff-necked, prune-mouthed dowager with nothing good to say to anyone?

She bit down on the insides of her cheeks to keep from saying anything more.

On her other side, Diana fidgeted, fussing with the ties to

the bonnet she had snatched up before Paxten had dragged them out of the inn.

Alexandria's temper flared. "Can you not sit still?" she snapped, frowning at her niece.

Diana stilled, then muttered, "I beg your pardon."

But then she was twisting again, and almost bouncing in her seat. "Was that not the most exciting thing? I thought for a certainty that we were caught. And to have to run from house to house—how did you know how do to that, Mr. Marsett?"

He started to answer, glanced at Alexandria, and then said, "Practice at the wrong sorts of things. You should forget you ever had to do such a thing."

"Oh, but it was just what we needed! And then to find a farmer just harnessing his gig, and to practically snatch it out from him!"

"Not exactly a godsend," Alexandria remarked, her tone dry. She glanced at the mismatched pair of horses—one brown, the other a roan. Heavy animals with thick, unruly manes, they looked as if they ought to be pulling a plow. As to the gig . . . "This vehicle has no springs, and we are like to be bounced to death in it."

"We won't be in it long enough," Paxten said. He had switched to speaking English as soon as they gained the open road, but now Alexandria stared at him, not comprehending him in the least.

"Won't be—? After you gave away my favorite brooch to buy this . . . this . . . carriage, you say we will not be in it that long? Are we that near the coast?"

"We are if you can fly. But, no, what I had in mind when I spoke is that those soldiers will be busy only a short while taking apart that inn. They may follow after your coach, but when they catch it, they'll realize they were tricked. And that will lead them back to that inn we left so quickly. Sooner or later, they will search that village."

Alexandria sat back for a moment, frowning. "You think they will talk to the farmer who sold us this gig?"

"Perhaps. If they do, the man might not want to talk about the brooch given him, but there are ways a man can be persuaded into talking."

Diana leaned forward to glance at him from the other side of Alexandria, her expression worried. "Persuaded—do you mean as in using force?"

Paxten lifted one shoulder, then winced. "Perhaps only threats. In any case, we are best served if we take the chance out of it. Which means we need to acquire another means of transport—and new identities."

Diana's eyes brightened. "Really? Oh, may I disguise myself as a boy and wear breeches?"

Alexandria gave her niece a withering stare. "My dear, if you put on breeches, a boy's figure is the last thing any man will think about. With your curves, you are more likely to begin a riot, so, no, you may not disguise yourself as a boy."

Diana's face fell. Alexandria turned her stare back to the road and the wide, mismatched rumps of the horses pulling the gig. She felt like the worst spoilsport. She put a hand on her niece's leg. "Now, I suppose I could make a perfectly adequate boy, what with my lack of curves."

Paxten glanced at her, an odd light in his eyes. "I should like to see you try."

She blushed hot, and since she could think of nothing to answer his remark, she glared at him and asked, "What did you really do to Lisette D'Aeth to bring so much wrath down on your head?"

"Only what I told you—but I am certain she gave her husband a story of the worst crimes. Ironic that I am now hunted for a sin I did not commit, when I have so many others waiting judgment."

Diana leaned forward to glance at Paxten around Alexandria. "Madame D'Aeth—so that is your Lisette! Whatever did you see in her? I always thought her rather common actually."

Paxten opened his mouth to answer, but Alexandria interrupted. "Diana, you will forget that you heard anything mentioned about Madame D'Aeth, and you will not repeat that comment, please."

"But I won't forget." Alexandria turned to glare at her niece, and the girl smiled back. "I mean, of course I should never dream of mentioning it to Father, or to Mummy for that matter—oh, wouldn't she just faint if I brought up anything so indelicate? But I am hardly a child. And if you can speak to Mr. Marsett of such matters, why can I not? Is not honest conversation of any value anywhere?"

Paxten grinned. "Not in the salons of Paris or London, but we are in the French countryside. And we are about to become solid French citizens, at one with the land and the seasons."

Diana's eyes brightened. "That sounds lovely. How do we do that?"

Inside, Alexandria groaned. Now he had her niece under his spell. And she could not think that his next idea would be any better than the last. But he was right. They needed to do all they could to throw off the trail of that captain and his men.

Why, she wondered, had she not set him down from her carriage at the very outset of this? She would certainly never forgive herself if her weakness for him led Diana into further danger.

Alexandria held up the rough cotton shift and the high-waisted dark-brown dress and stared at them. On the ground lay a straw bonnet, wool stockings with plain garters to tie them up, and sturdy half-boots. Behind her, a stream gurgled over pebbles, rocks, and fallen branches in a light rush of sound. A breeze whispered through the trees overhead, and dappled sunlight shifted across the spring grass and dark earth.

A longing for her own gowns tightened in her chest. Soft silks and bold satins. Lace so fine that it seemed tatted from a fairy's web. Soft muslin designed to float and spin as one danced. Kid gloves made to fit perfect, satin dancing slippers and boots so soft, the leather molded to her feet. All gone.

Well, she had the lawn chemise she wore, the material so fine as to be nearly transparent. And soft. She would keep that. And her corset. And her own silk stockings. Perhaps she could wash them in the stream nearby. And she could still use her own pink satin garters trimmed in lace. And her boots.

That left the horrid dress. And the bonnet.

She glanced around her.

Paxten had left them at the edge of a wooded area, near a thick stand of beech trees and not far from a narrow, fast stream fed by a spring. Flowers of some sort—small and white—bloomed in the shade. She had never known the name of any plant other than a rose and a lily.

"Best if you're not seen in town when I sell the gig," he had said. Alexandria had winced at the effort it took him to climb back into the carriage.

"I ought to come with you," she told him.

With a smile, he shook his head. "And have your description left behind for those soldiers to follow? The idea here is to hide our tracks, and I cannot do that with a lady beside me."

She had frowned at that, wanting to argue, but he had driven off before she could come up with better reasons for his needing her assistance.

He returned an hour later, riding the roan without a saddle but with two cloth bags slung before him over the horse's withers. After sliding from the roan's back, he pulled the bags down and opened one, producing a wine bottle, thick-crusted bread wrapped in a cloth, cheese covered in red wax, and sweet green apples.

Ravenous, she had eaten like a peasant, sitting on the ground, drinking the wine—a sharp red that tasted of oak and spices—from the bottle, letting Paxten entertain them with the story of his horse trading.

"Is that all you got for the gig?" she said, outraged when he counted the few coins from his leather purse.

"No, it's not, but I spent some of it." He pulled out the clothes from the other bag. "For you, Mistress Marsett, and for you, Mademoiselle Marsett. We are now the Marsett family, en route to Boulogne to see our lovely daughter here wed to a fisherman's son she met last year while we were visiting cousins. And scowl you may, Andria, for you are to be the wife who dislikes the marriage and therefore says little. You should be able to manage that with your French."

She lifted one eyebrow. "You could teach me to curse."

"I may just. Now, if you will excuse me, I've a horse to sell and other transport to arrange."

With a grin he started back to the horse. Alexandria followed him. "You were supposed to be in bed today."

He had been gathering up the reins to the bridle, but he paused and turned to her. His color had gone pale again, and a sheen lay on his skin. She wanted to touch her hand to his face and decided that she could risk that much. So she brushed the back of her fingers across his forehead. Not too warm. No fever. But he looked so tired.

He caught her hand, and his thumb brushed the inside of her wrist. "Worried for me?"

She jerked away from his hold. "If you collapse while away, you leave us stranded here, so, yes, I am worried!" She sounded as sharp as a shrew, but he did not seem to mind.

He grinned. "Ah, but how could I stay away from two beautiful women, even if I had to return as a ghost?"

"Please do not joke about that."

"Then give me a leg up, if you like. Or do you care to ride before me on this old roan? I cannot swear she will take both our weights, however, even though you are still almost as slim as a girl."

She glanced at the horse, then at him. "You have an annoying habit of being right about things. How do I give you a leg up?"

He had to coach her in how to grab his left leg when he bent it, one hand wrapped around his knee and the other at his ankle. It brought her closer to him than when she had been sitting in the gig with him, and the awareness of him tingled on her skin.

The first time she did not boost enough, and he glared at her. "I'm not china to break!"

The next time, she lifted hard on his count of three, and he almost sailed over the horse's back. Catching the mane with one hand, he grinned down at her. Then he reached out and twirled a lock of her hair around his fingers. He gave a tug on it and let go. "I'd kiss you if I could do so without slipping off this beast. Make yourself pretty for me while I'm gone."

But how could anyone be pretty in these clothes?

She nearly jumped as a twig snapped behind her, and she turned to see Diana.

"Look at me, Aunt! Do you think Father would even know me now?"

The girl twirled, looking like a wood nymph in the small clearing. Alexandria shook her head.

Diana had let down her hair, and the golden curls fell to the middle of her back. She had on a simple blue muslin gown, high-waisted, with a yellow scarf tucked into the neckline. It looked appropriate for Marie-Jeanne, not a young lady of birth who had only a few weeks earlier graced the grandest salons of Paris.

Skipping forward, Diana picked up the sleeve of her aunt's dress, holding it out. "I suppose he did not get you as pretty a gown, but if you are supposed to be my glowering *mère* . . ." She glanced at her aunt.

The poor dear had not been happy about leaving their things behind, and Diana almost gave a sigh herself for the dresses she had bought in Paris and left at the inn. Such pretty things, and all in the latest fashion. It would have been lovely to take them home and show them off. However, far better to have a story to tell.

So how did she coax her aunt into a better humor so that she did not spoil this most amazing experience?

She put an arm around her aunt. "You know we could ask him to get you something a bit more . . . well, more scandalous. You could be disguised as his mistress, and I could be the daughter who disapproves."

Her aunt snatched the dress from Diana's hands. "I am not Lady Scandal."

Diana's face warmed. She had not meant to bring this up, but since her aunt had mentioned it, she decided she might as well use the opportunity.

Stepping around to undo the ties at the back of her aunt's lovely gold-patterned gown, Diana asked, "Of course you are not, Aunt. But something must have occurred to cause you to once be known as Lady Scandal."

Eight

"It was years ago," her aunt said, her voice as closed as her expression. She then dropped the cotton shift, slipped out of her gold gown, and busied herself in pulling on the brown.

Before she had it so much as up over her knees, Diana stopped her. "Really, now! How will you ever look the part proper if you do not wear everything?"

"I am not going to itch in uncomfortable undergarments."

"What if we are stopped and searched? There might be any number of barricades that have been set up along the way to catch fleeing English. And the ports are bound to be full of soldiers!"

Her aunt frowned, glanced at the clothes, then gave a sigh. "Oh, very well."

Smiling, Diana started to help again, undoing the laces to her aunt's corset. "I suppose what you did could not have been all that scandalous, for I have never heard so much as a breath of it. Still, I suppose Father would know—"

"No!"

Diana blinked.

Her aunt had turned positively red. Now she fussed with slipping out of her light corset and chemise and into the rough linen, hurrying with the changing. "I beg your pardon," she muttered as she dressed. "I do not mean to be harsh about it. But I wish the past left where it is. That means I will not discuss it now, and you are not to ask your father about it if . . . when we return home."

Diana frowned. Honestly, her aunt could be so stubborn at times. Plucking the straw bonnet from the ground, she studied it. "Yes, but, dear, do you really think the past will stay in the past what with Mr. Marsett now with us every moment of the day?"

"It had better. Now help me get the rest of these ghastly clothes on."

Subdued, Diana did so.

Alexandria found that they fit better than she had thought they would. The dress, far from being shapeless, clung tight around the bodice and had been cut close in the skirt, probably to save the cost of fabric. The results revealed her narrow waist and the curve of her hips and pushed up her breasts. She had not felt so well endowed since she was pregnant. It seemed a dress to suit a Lady Scandal after all.

She turned, and then glanced at Diana. The girl's eyes sparkled with delight. "Why, no one in London would know you!"

"I am not certain of that. Still . . ." Reaching up, she started to pull the pins from her hair. Diana moved forward at once to help.

Her hair was not as long as Diana's, but she had not had it trimmed since they had arrived in France. Once loose, it brushed her shoulders. She pulled a section from the front on each side, then asked Diana to take the ribbon from the straw bonnet and use it to tie up the strands.

Then she glanced at her white hands and at Diana's. "Neither of us look as if we have done a day's work in our lives, which is just about the truth."

Picking up a handful of dirt, she scrubbed her hands with it and then Diana's. "This will not produce appropriate calluses, but I hope we may avoid such close inspection."

Diana wrinkled her nose, then she laughed. "I have not been allowed to play in the dirt since I was five."

Giving her a stern glance, Alexandria shook her head. "This is not play. I do not know what those soldiers intend for

Paxten if they find him, but it cannot be good. And I doubt it will go well for us either. Not when we have been aiding him. Keep that in mind."

Her warning sobered the girl, and Alexandria almost wished she had not needed to be so plainspoken. But it would not do to make this into some May-game. Not with the stakes so high.

They settled under the beech trees to wait for Paxten. The sun fell lower, pulling long shadows from the trees. The breeze shifted to the north and took on a chill so that Diana hugged herself against it. And they saw nothing more than a farmer bent over on a donkey cart, slowly making his way along the winding dirt lane.

Alexandria alternated between inventing pictures of Paxten collapsed along the roadside and worrying that perhaps he intended to leave them in the woods. The Paxten she had known could never have done such a thing, but she was not certain that man still existed. At times she had thought she had glimpsed him, but was that the truth, or her own wishful thinking?

Still, she had her jewels, or most of them, with her. If need be, she could manage without him. But what if he had not managed so well on his own? She ought never to have allowed him to go off without her.

And then she realized that the farmer bent over the donkey cart had veered off the road and was heading toward them.

It was Paxten.

As he neared, he looked up. Under the black slouch hat pulled low, she recognized his handsome face with its strong nose and dark eyes. He had exchanged the footman's black breeches and coat and stiff white shirt for tan breeches and an open-necked muslin shirt with billowing sleeves. With a plain black waistcoat, white stockings, and sturdy black shoes, he looked almost a peasant. Almost. That face—finely made with wide, intelligent eyes and aristocratic nose—belonged to no peasant. He might, however, pass for a brigand dressed as he was. No wonder he wore that hat pulled low.

She wondered if her own disguise and Diana's were as thin. Did they look like a farm wife and a maid? Or like the aristocrats who had once fled this land and the guillotine?

In the golden twilight, Diana bounced to her feet and hurried forward. "A donkey! How adorable! Can I drive him?"

"I think Maximilian has gone far enough for the day," Paxten said, halting the cart and easing himself from it. He moved with care, Alexandria noted, and if his face had looked pale before, now it seemed drained of color and tight with new lines.

Because of that, she held back her irritation. A donkey cart of all things! What would he be putting them in next? A dung wagon? She certainly ought to have gone with him, only for different reasons than she had thought earlier. But when had she ever persuaded him to reasonable actions?

Diana petted the donkey's face and then drew the long ears between her fingertips. The donkey seemed to like the attention well enough, or at least it stood placid in its traces. The two-wheeled cart attached to it had a wooden bench seat and a canvas covering over what looked to be a flat area for storage.

"Care to help with the harness, and then take Maximilian to water?" Paxten asked the girl.

"Oh, can I? But I can manage on my own. I used to have a cart at home with the sweetest pair of cream ponies. Father always says that a horsewoman must be able to care for her mounts as well as any groom or she is nothing more than a passenger."

"You've a wise father."

"Terribly so. You have no idea how dull it is. Come along, Maximilian—such a mouthful of name for such a darling little thing." Diana unbuckled the harness with efficient moves that showed her familiarity with the task, and then led the donkey to the nearby stream, talking to it the whole time as if it were an old friend.

Paxten smiled at her. Was there anything as energetic as youth? Had he ever been young? Pressing a hand to his aching side, he decided no. Then he turned to see Alexandria staring at him, wearing her disapproving face, with her lips taut and gray eyes storming.

"Is it the donkey, or something else?" he asked, his tone cautious.

"The donkey—and you. You look exhausted. I do not know how we shall get you to an inn tonight."

"No need. I've brought the bed to you—*voilà!*" He drew back the canvas covering on the cart as he spoke, revealing blankets, pillows, and a basket from which the aroma of a meat pie teased.

She stared at him, dismay in her eyes. "You mean there is to be no roof over our heads?"

"We had best avoid any more inns, for they leave too easy a trail to follow."

No inns? No beds? Her mind struggled to grasp such a concept, and then the urge to sit down and cry swept into her. Tears burned the back of her eyes and stung her nose. Shocked at herself, she turned away. He was beside her in an instant, his arm around her waist, his wide shoulders temptingly close. "Ah, what is it, *ma petite chou?* Is it the donkey cart you so dislike?"

She longed to lean against him and give in to this absurd weakness. She had not known until just an instant before how much she had been looking forward to a hot meal and a bed and . . . and oh, how ridiculous she must look to be nearly crying over such trivialities.

Sniffling, she stepped away. "I beg your pardon. It is nothing—nothing, except that I am tired and hungry, and . . . and I thought you were lying dead beside the road, or that you would not come back at all, and I . . . oh, it is nonsensical, but I've never slept on the ground, and it sounds so uncomfortable!"

He closed on her again. She batted his hands away, but still he gathered her in his arms and pulled her head against his chest, muttering things in French that she did not understand.

She sniffled again. She ought not to stand in his arms, her control threatening to come undone and his hand stroking her hair. It did no good for his injury. And he had probably held that Lisette of his just so only a few days before—horrible woman that she was. And . . . and what if Diana returned to see this?

Her mind whirled.

But she stayed in the shelter of his arms, eyes closed, letting that lovely rumble of his voice pour over her. Her arms stole around him. Perhaps just a few moments. She let out a ragged breath. It had been such a long day.

Tightening his arms, Paxten rested his head on hers and closed his eyes. His poor Andria. Never to have slept under the stars, nor to have had the joy of sturdy clothing that could be worn without a care, nor to have traveled anywhere without an army of servants to both see to her and hem her in at the same time. So much that was new—too much perhaps.

And *she* had been worried for *him.*

He smiled.

He ought to use this, he knew. He had been looking for her to show some vulnerability, to show some flaw he could exploit, and now that she had, he wanted only to hold her and tell her that it would be all right.

Ah, what a lie that was. What was ever right in this world? Least of all him. Or anything between them?

He knew the moment she relaxed, felt the stiffness slip away from that slim, straight back, heard her breath come easier and soft now.

Leaning away from her, he looked down and brushed a strand of hair from her face. The setting sun turned her hair into a nimbus of gold around her head. He had wanted her hair loose, and now he remembered how it curved around that strong chin. He cupped her face with one hand. She had her eyes closed still, and her lips parted as if expecting the kiss he intended. Ah, so she knew him too, it seemed. How easily they fell into this reading of each other.

He started to bend to her, then he heard Diana's light chatter.

Alexandria must have heard it too, for she bolted from his hold, the languor of a moment ago vanished into that brisk English tone of hers. "I suppose if we are to camp tonight, we shall need a fire. I certainly hope you know how to make one, for I have no idea."

The corner of his mouth tightened. The practical Lady Sandal had returned. Well, he could wait. He had what he needed—that small opening. He could work on that, widen it. Play on her concern for him. And when the moment arrived, he would know just how to shatter the protection she wore around her heart. He would then make certain that his Lady Scandal truly earned the name he had given her.

By the time he had a fire built, he had exhausted the last of his strength. Diana and Alexandria had gathered wood at his direction, coming back with small armfuls. He almost went off to handle the task himself, but he knew his limits. He had reached them. So he used what few branches they brought, then he pulled out the blankets from the cart, and prayed for fair weather.

Diana's bright voice filled the evening as they ate the meat pie. The fire crackled bright before them, doing more to cheer them than it did to warm. The girl was a wonder. She seemed to mind nothing. How had anyone in Alexandria's starched family ever spawned such a changeling? He had met Alexandria's younger brother, a bookish fellow with no interest in anything much beyond the towers of Oxford. But Alexandria's parents had pushed him into society, as they had their daughter. Alexandria's brother had dutifully gone and married as his family arranged. Ah, how well Alexandria's parents matched his own cold-blooded English relatives.

As if echoing his thoughts of family, Diana asked suddenly, "Were your parents *émigrés,* Mr. Marsett?"

He glanced at the girl, her face pale in the firelight, her hair glimmering and bright. "If you mean did they flee the Revolution as did so many, then no. My mother was English, and my father was dead long before the old regime vanished."

"Oh, I am sorry."

He smiled and stretched out beside the fire, lying on his good side to ease the ache on the other. "Nothing to regret in that, *ma petite fille*. He was sixty when he married my mother, and he died in his bed ten years later—a happy man, I expect."

"Really, Paxten!"

At Alexandria's prim words he grinned at her. "Yes, really. Her family, however, did not find such a marriage so nice. A Frenchman, an older Frenchman, shocked them, I think. Even if he had land and titles—and he did. She had a child—me, of course—and had no idea how to manage without him, so she went back to England. Then came the Revolution, and the land and titles went."

Diana leaned forward, and firelight flickered over the concern on her face. "How awful. Have you never wanted to get them back?"

He drank the last of the wine from the bottle. "Ah, but to do so I would have to become of use to the current ruling power—that means Bonaparte. And I think the only use he might have for a half-English Frenchman is as a spy."

"That's ghastly!"

She sounded so genuinely appalled that he smiled. "But pragmatic, is it not? The First Consul has ever been that. It is, however, too much work for my taste. Besides, my English cousins pay me well enough to stay far away from London, and so I do."

"They pay you . . . but that is absurd."

"Why? They dislike the scandal I stirred up, and they want to make certain I do not come back to embarrass them more. Trying to force a man into a duel is not a nice thing after all. But then, neither is trying to run off with his wife."

"Thank you, Paxten, I think we have heard enough on such an old and tired topic," Alexandria said, her words clipped.

"Oh, but *I* haven't," Diana protested. "It sounds fascinating."

"There, you see, Andria. Why do you not tell her your part of that old and tired topic? Surely it can serve as a moral lesson if nothing else."

"There is no lesson to give, thank you very much. Diana, if you must know the story, Mr. Marsett and I shared a . . . a flirtation."

"Ah, yes, we did nothing but play cards."

Alexandria shot him a warning stare. "There was talk, but there always is talk in London."

"And there was that duel that did not happen—by the saints, I have never seen a man so determined to talk his way out of a duel as was your Bertram. I nearly shot him on the spot just to make him stop talking."

Diana frowned. "But that would have been terribly unsporting."

"*Ma fille,* I did not harbor sporting feelings toward Lord Sandal. He was a bore. And a—"

"Thank you, Paxten, for your kind assessment of my late husband."

He grinned. "Come, Andria, you never loved him either. You ought to be at least that honest with us—and yourself."

"That may be, but I also do not care to malign him now that he is passed on and unable to defend himself."

"Ah, but he was unable, or unwilling, to defend himself when alive." He turned back to Diana. "The blunt truth, *ma fille,* is that your aunt nearly ran off with me."

Diana smiled. "Really? How wonderfully romantic."

He shook his head. "No, not very. The word to remark is *nearly.* She made the practical choice, not the romantic one. And—"

Alexandria's voice cut across his flippant tone. "I had a son to consider!"

Paxten sat up, the amusement gone from him. "Your son

wasn't your reason to stay—he was your excuse! Admit it. The boy was already gone from you! He was sent to Eton. You had nothing to hold you except that you could not give up your title and position! You let duty chain you to them!"

She glared at him, firelight reflected hot in her eyes. "I stayed to keep my son from being shamed by me."

He met her stare, eyes black and shadowed, and his voice dropped to a growl. "You lied to me once. Do not expect another lie to find a home with me."

The fire crackled. Sparks flew to the stars overhead. Paxten kept his stare locked on Alexandria, his eyes narrowed. Even in the light of the flame, he could see the patches of angry red on her cheeks.

Diana rose suddenly, hugging herself, her face shadowed but strain in her voice as she spoke. "Do you know, I think I shall go to bed. I've a pillow and blanket in the back of the cart. Good night, Aunt, Mr. Marsett." She dropped a quick curtsy and scooted away into the darkness to where Paxten had left the cart, its shafts propped up to keep the bed in the back of it flat.

Blinking, Alexandria pushed a hand through her hair and looked away from Paxten. Now they had made a scene in front of Diana. How did the man manage to bring out the worst in her? And why was she attempting to defend a position that proved her right for having had to hurt him?

"I beg your pardon," she muttered, staring at the fire.

For a moment he said nothing, then his voice came to her, sounding as weary as she felt. "No, I should beg yours." He gave a dry chuckle and she glanced at him. "Every time I promise myself I shall behave, and then I cannot wait to claw at you. Ah, but perhaps you were right not to come with me back then."

She wet her lips, then said, her voice soft, "I wanted to."

He said nothing.

She tucked her feet close to her and rested her chin on her knees. "I had even packed my things that night, to leave with you just as we planned."

His voice came out of the darkness, low and rough, but without accusation, just resignation. "And then you changed your mind."

Pausing, she drew in a breath. She kept her stare fixed on the fire, seeing not the flames but her younger self. A girl really, unhappy in her marriage and in love with a dashing young man whom she adored. He was right. Her son had gone off to Eton the year before. The parting had been one of the things that had left her life so hollow, and herself so vulnerable to Paxten. So needing of someone who might care for her.

Now she needed him to understand, as he had not been able to when last they parted.

"Yes. Yes, I did. Perhaps I ought to have pleaded a headache so that I could have gone to my rooms and then left at once, but I had to be the hostess that Bertram wanted—there to greet everyone. To make the circuit around the room with Bertram. He always went into the card room as soon as he could after that, and I thought I could leave then."

She pressed her lips tight. Sap popped in the fire. She shook her head. "He seemed not to have a sense of anything being different. I was terrified he might. Not for fear he would make a scene. Chetwynds do not make scenes you know. But I feared he would discover my intent and simply refuse to allow it. He could do that. Just pretend it did not exist. I had this irrational idea he would do that with me—have me carried off to one of his country estates and simply shut me up and forget me. But he said nothing, just smiled at everyone as we went around. And then he went into the card room. And I left to meet you."

"To tell me good-bye, you mean."

She swallowed hard and could not look at him. She could not face the anguish she heard in his voice, could not bear to see it on his face.

"That was not my intent, even then. I—oh, it is no excuse, and I do not expect forgiveness. I cannot forgive myself. But

I cannot change it either. I stopped to look at myself in the mirror. I wanted to look beautiful for you. And so I stopped to fuss with my hair and make certain my necklace lay straight. I had on the topaz that you had given me. You know, Bertram never even noticed other than to remark that I ought to buy myself yellow diamonds instead of such shabby gems."

She shook her head, the heartache so old, so faded, but still there. Such a silly little thing. Was that how one's life always changed? By an instant when the world shifted?

"I heard them talking as I stood there. I do not even know who they were other than they were two of the usual catty sorts one meets in London. Gossiping away as ever."

"About you?"

"About Jules actually. Do you know, I had thought it poetic fiction that one could be held still by fury. But I could not move for the anger. I could only listen to them go on and on about the 'poor boy' and how awful it would be for him. They, of course, had sensed something. Bertram had not seen it in me, but they had.

" 'Do you think she'll run off with him?' one of them said," she said, mimicking the voices she had overheard that night. " 'Oh, Lady Scandal—of course she will. But it will be little Lord Scandal who grows up to bear his mother's shame.' "

She broke off the story, for her throat had thickened. How did she put into words the agony that had filled her? The shame. She had seen exactly what her son would endure if she put her desire first. The gossip. The taunting. And he was already so withdrawn and isolated. So different from other boys. If only she had had other children, who . . .

There she was again, deep in regret.

She had not been able to do it. Perhaps she ought to have. Perhaps she should have kidnapped Jules from Eton and fled with Paxten. He could hardly have been more neglectful as a stepfather than Bertram had proved as a father.

But her courage had faltered.

"Even then, I still intended to meet you. I sent a maid for my cloak. But when I saw your coach outside, I . . . oh, I am sorry."

The fire was dying. Hot embers glowed but the flames flickered low. She could not bear to bring up that horrid scene between them. She had thrown on her cloak and had gone out to tell him she could not leave—and his anger ignited her own. They had been so awful to each other that night, flinging accusations at each other.

She had struck him even. She closed her eyes.

Paxten's voice drifted to her, quiet, but without the rancor that had once tainted his words. "You gave me so many promises before that night."

Opening her eyes, she looked at him. "I did. And I kept none of them. And I ought to have given you more patience. More kindness. I knew you had to leave."

He shook his head. "Yes, but I brought that on us by trying to force Sandal into that duel—was there ever such a mad notion as that? I knew my cousin would not tolerate it. But I went ahead anyway. And, of course, so did he."

"So it was your cousin who gave you the idea that you must leave England. I thought as much."

"It was not so much an idea. He told me to book passage or he would arrange matters. And I had no wish to wake up one morning in the bowels of some ship, possibly in chains."

"Good heavens! No wonder you sounded so desperate that last night. Why did you not tell me then?"

"Ah, but I did not want my lack of choice forced on you. I wanted you to come because you would, not because I had to go. And you had said you would. Besides, what would it have changed?"

Nothing. Nothing.

She shook her head. "I am sorry. So very sorry. It seems I cannot say that enough. But why did you never return? You told me once that if we had to part, you would come back to me. That you would wait until I had my freedom." She

winced as she heard the desperation in her voice—she
sounded so much like a woman in love still. She had not been
that for years.

He laughed. Her mouth tightened. She could have hit him
for finding cynical humor in this when she had shown him
her scars. Then he sobered. "*Ma chère,* I meant that divorce
you said you would ask for from him, and which you never
did."

"Oh, I asked! I demanded it. It nearly gave him heart failure when I did. His answer, when he could speak again, was
that Chetwynds did not divorce. He then refused to speak of
it again."

Scorn laced his words. "How polite of you to ask. You
could have sought a divorce from him, *ma chère.*"

"On what grounds?"

"That he was no real husband to you. Or you could have
made such a public scandal, my Lady Scandal, that he would
have been delighted to see you gone."

A half-burned branch shifted on the fire, sputtering into the
dirt. Was he right? Had she not tried hard enough? Perhaps.
She rubbed a hand across her eyes. Perhaps she ought to have
put their love before everything. Only she had not been able
to do so.

She glanced at him, at his dark eyes and pale face, at the
burning light in those eyes and the hard set to his jaw. Could
she at least make it easier for him? Could she give up trying
to make him the villain for having to do what he must? She
wet her lips. "You are right. I failed you. You needed someone who loved you more than I ever did."

Paxten glared at her. The admission, the words he had so
long wanted to wrench from her, thudded into him like lead.
Impatient with her—and with himself—he stood. Diana had
the right of it—they all ought to have been in bed hours ago.

As he rose, he forgot his injury. His sudden movement
pulled an ache from his side and startled a gasp from him. He
stood still to ease the pain, and at once Alexandria was there,

hardly more than a shadow in the darkness but holding on to him, and concern in her voice again. "Do you need that bandage changed? Is it wrapped too tight? We ought to have had it off while there was light still. I can—"

"Merde," he muttered, choking out the word on a dry laugh, and then he put his arms around her and kissed her.

Nine

So you did not love me enough? he thought as his mouth covered hers. His arms closed around her, trapping her. She did not struggle in his hold and he almost wanted her to. He wanted the excuse to force her to face the truth. To make her see. He intended to prove her a liar once and always with him.

Then her lips parted.

He forgot what he had intended to prove. Forgot words: things said or wished unsaid. He forgot things done or left undone. Everything vanished into the hot taste of her, the soft moan pulled from her as she gave to him, the scent of her like spiced flowers.

His hands closed on her waist. He wanted to drag her down to the ground. Wanted hot skin pressed to hot skin, and her trembling, and the pleasure they could give to each other with only the stars to see and the grass to hold them. He wanted other memories, not the bitter ones that lay between them. Not the hurt they had given each other.

By instinct he started to sink down, pulling her with him, but as he bent, a brand of pain flashed up his side. With a gasp, he broke the kiss to put a hand on his injury, muttering curses in French and holding her with his other hand to steady himself.

"That must be seen to," she said, her voice thick with passion but with a firm hand now taking hold of his.

"There's no need."

"I have tended a son through falls from his first horse and

childhood ailments, so I ought to be able to manage a fresh bandage for you."

He recognized the stubborn tone, so he submitted to sitting down for her and undoing the cloth ties of his shirt to let the muslin hang open. The night air wrapped a chill around him, but the cooling did him good. It made him able to think again, or almost so.

And to curse his unsteady temper. When would he ever learn to be patient and wait for the right time for anything?

She found more wood for the fire and tossed a dry branch onto the embers. As yellow flames licked upward, she went to rummage through the supplies he had bought that sat beside the cart. She came back with her own fine lawn chemise in hand. "This will at least be soft on your skin. Now let's untie the ends of that bandage."

He smiled at that. He liked the idea of something she had worn now pressed to his skin, her scent wrapping around him.

She focused on her task, frowning as she worked. The firelight played over one side of her face, while the darkness cloaked the other side of her. He leaned back on his hands and allowed her to work, too tired to protest, unable to remember when anyone had last shown him such tenderness. His mother had not been one to do so, for she had swooned over so much as a bruise and left his care mostly to nursemaids. She had adored, however, dressing him as fine as she should could, something he had loathed as a boy. His English cousins had teased him horribly over the lace at his throat and wrists, and his velvet suits. And over his faint accent. And for every other thing that had marked him as different. Later, he had enjoyed throwing every convention he could find back into their faces with his defiance of it and his disdain of them.

He let out a soft sigh. "Ah, *ma chère,* why are we so bad for each other? I drag you into this, and now you are left having to patch me. And after being so rude to you tonight as well."

She struggled and found a smile. "At least you know to bring a decent meal back with you. How long do you think it will take us to reach Boulogne in that donkey cart of yours—must we really travel in that contraption?"

"It's safer. Even more so if we stay to the back roads. Have you thought as well that we could make for Dieppe from here? It's not so far."

She glanced at him. "But Dieppe makes for a very long crossing to England."

He smiled. "You sound like a cat who does not like the water."

"Cats are sensible creatures. And if you had spent your last crossing hanging over a ship's railing, you might think twice about extending the time you must bob about in the water."

He grinned at her, then winced as she pulled the bandage from his skin. He glanced down. A red gash of perhaps four inches, puffy and deep enough to scar, cut horizontally over his ribs. He had enough vanity that the fact it would forever mar his side irritated him. "Well, at least it no longer bleeds."

"Yes, but I do not like that swelling or the redness. Did you bring any powders back with you?"

"A visit to any apothecary seemed as good as leaving my calling card to be found—those soldiers know I've been shot."

"We shall have to make do with charred wood then."

He pulled back. "Wood? Since when do you know how to heal, and where did you hear such a wives' tale?"

"From a wife. A midwife, actually. I did my lying-in with Jules in the countryside and not with a London doctor. My aunt's advice, and she is someone who knows about these things—she has had eight girls and three boys. The midwife quite shocked me by blackening her hands. But she claimed she never had a lady or child brought to bed with fever after any birth because of it."

"If it is good enough to suit my lady, by all means, blacken me like a moor."

By the time Alexandria had his injury tended and bandaged again—using strips of her chemise—she wanted only to collapse. The fire had burned down again, but she had no energy to rebuild it. Paxten, too, she guessed, must be exhausted.

She noticed how careful they were now with their words, keeping to topics without deep feelings in them.

That kiss, however, lingered between them, making her far too aware of him, and of her own body's ache for him. And so she avoided looking at him as much as she could, and did not meet his dark-eyed gaze. She might lose herself in that darkness. Besides, they needed rest. So she found them both blankets and pillows, and then she pulled off her shoes and lay down on the ground.

Within minutes, she started to shiver. The earth seemed to suck the heat from her. She twisted, trying to find comfort. A pebble dug into her back. She turned on her side. In the darkness, some animal rustled through the nearby woods. Something small, she hoped. Wings flapped above them—bats or owls? She shivered. And turned again.

Then she heard a soft mutter, like a caress of rough velvet. "You are keeping me awake with all that noise you make."

She frowned into the darkness in the direction of Paxten's deep voice. "I am sorry, but I am freezing."

"Come here."

At his order, propriety warred with physical need. She could not possibly lay with him. Sharing body heat did sound utterly sensible, however. And they were far indeed from anything that even resembled Society—so why heed its restrictions? Bundling her blanket and pillow into her arms, she eased her way in the darkness toward his voice.

"Spread your blanket down to lie on, then you may share mine over both of us."

His suggestion sounded indecent. But warm. So she did as he asked, careful of his injured side. Within moments he had his arms around her. Her arms nestled between them, elbows bent and her hands pressed against his chest. The warmth of him soaked into her.

"Better?" he mumbled against her temple, his voice already drifting.

She held herself still. "Yes. Thank you." Oh, heavens, what had she gotten into with this?

"*De rien.*" He muttered the words, trailing off.

She lay there, tense, uncertain, embarrassed.

How absurd was that? Who, after all, was there to see them lying with each other? And this was only a matter of practical comfort, after all.

Letting out a breath, she snuggled closer, and her lashes brushed his jaw as her eyes closed.

Birdsong woke Diana, light, soaring, bursting with life. She opened her eyes and lay in the back of the cart, her knees bent to fit. Sleep still held her arms and legs. But the world beckoned.

The air smelled of spring—flowers opening to scent the dawn and new grass pushing up through the warming ground. Slowly she stretched. Why did everyone shut themselves up under roofs rather than wake this way every day?

Sitting up, she poked her head from the back of the cart.

Then she stared, her jaw slackening.

Not ten paces from the cart, beside the charred remains of the fire, her aunt lay entwined with Mr. Marsett. Her aunt's skirt had ridden up, and her stockings had fallen to reveal a bare calf. Mr. Marsett's shirt lay open, and her aunt's hand rested lightly on his naked chest. A blanket twisted around their middles, hiding . . . well, it did not hide enough, Diana decided.

Ducking back into the cart, she lay down again. How charming they looked. She frowned. How ghastly they had been to each other last night.

Her parents fenced in just such a way—always seeking to wound the other with hard words. Not an enjoyable thing to live around, and she could not imagine it would be very nice to have to be a participant in such verbal battles.

Thankfully, her parents generally left their children out of such matters. They certainly left her out. An older sister—who was being presented to Society this year—and a younger brother, allowed her mostly to go unnoticed. She would never have been permitted to go to France, however, if either of her parents had thought she would end up sleeping in donkey carts and running away from soldiers. She had Henrietta's presentation to thank for that.

"Every gentleman who pays a call takes one look at you and cannot even see your sister!" her mother had complained.

Her father, of course, had not wanted her to go. He had thought it dangerous. He had protested that he would miss her too much. But her mother won the disagreement, as she did most quarrels. Father would certainly never let Mama forget that circumstances had proven him right.

Diana peeked out again at her aunt and Mr. Marsett. They had not moved. She rather liked how his head angled toward hers and how his arm lay around her aunt. So protective. Possessive almost. But did he really care for her?

She sat back again. She did not understand them. Love ought to soften the heart. It ought to be kind. And gentle.

An image of the French officer who had stopped their coach came to her then. There had been nothing gentle about that harsh, handsome face. Nor anything kind in his words or manner. Still, he had stopped his men from rifling through their things. And he had allowed them to leave. Kind acts certainly. And hidden under brusque words and a hard expression.

Was there also something hidden that she did not see between her aunt and Mr. Marsett?

She let out a sigh. Why could the world not be a simple place with everyone honest about their intentions? It seemed to her that most people did not even know why they acted as they did. Which meant that Aunt Alexandria needed a chaperone far more than she ever had.

Well, she could provide that for her aunt. After all, some danger on an adventure could be expected. But too much of anything violated the bounds of good taste.

She made a show of stretching, and thumping around in the cart to find her shoes, and of remarking loudly what a glorious day had dawned. By the time she swung down from the back of the cart, Mr. Marsett had vanished and her aunt stood near the dead fire embers, running her fingers through the tangle of her hair.

She smiled at once, but with her cheeks flushed. "Good morning, dear, I trust you slept well? I believe Mr. Marsett has gone to fetch us water. Do we have any apples left for breakfast?"

They had no apples. Nor much of anything else to eat. Paxten advised them to drink a good deal of water. "It fills the belly," he said, then gave Diana a wink.

She frowned at him.

By the time the sun had risen high, she had forgotten to disapprove of him and instead begged, "Can we not stop somewhere for a meal? I am famished!"

Alexandria gave her niece a smile, but her empty stomach echoed the sentiments. The cart rumbled along under them, Paxten's hands loose on the rein and the donkey proving remarkably quick in its walk. They had seen nothing more of anything resembling soldiers, but then, they had avoided anything but open countryside.

Abruptly, Alexandria straightened. "Look. There must be a farmhouse or village ahead—you can see the smoke there above the trees. Paxten, do let us stop. After all, we cannot not eat again until we reach England."

He argued against stopping but finally gave into Alexandria and Diana's joint protests. "But, mind, we halt only if the smoke proves to come from a single farmhouse. And I will do the talking for us. Now do your best to look like poor peasants."

"We have the starving part down quite well," Diana answered, her tone pert.

Alexandria smiled. Despite her hunger, despite the sore muscles from having slept on the ground, she had never felt so happy. So lighthearted. Was it that she had at last been able to tell Paxten everything? Or was it just having slept in his arms?

Her face warmed at that, but she could summon no guilt. Not when she had enjoyed it so much. But she knew better than to take it as anything other than what it was—a pleasant memory now, and nothing to indicate any hope for the future.

Remember that only a few days ago he had someone else in his arms.

But had he really called another woman by her name?

Satisfaction curled inside her. She could not stop it. However, she knew enough to recognize the danger of pride in such a dubious accomplishment. Still, how nice that he had not been able to forget her.

The smoke she had glimpsed came indeed from a rough farmhouse. The thatched roof needed repair. The stained walls had yellowed from mud and rain and needed whitewash. The gray stone fence around a pen of recently shorn sheep had rocks missing from its jagged top.

In the yard, a dark-haired woman dressed in black scowled at them as Paxten drew the cart to a halt. Four thin black chickens clucked and scratched the dirt around her, heads bobbing as they pecked at the ground. With weathered skin and her lined face, the woman might have been seventy or a badly aged fifty. Her mouth pulled down and black eyes glared at them as Paxten gave her a cheerful *bonjour*.

Easing himself from the cart, Paxten handed the reins to Alexandria and strode across the yard to converse with the woman. Alexandria quickly lost track of his rapid French. She started to look around her but straightened and looked back when the woman burst out with an angry tirade.

Leaning close to her niece, Alexandria asked, "What is it? Did he offend her?"

"I . . . well, she seems to be insulted by his offer to pay for food. She is going on and on that even with her husband and sons away in the army she needs no such charity."

"Oh, dear. She is proud." Alexandria glanced at the chickens, thinking longingly of how good an omelet would taste. Such a delicacy now seemed unlikely, unless . . .

She turned to Diana. "Perhaps there is another approach that would serve better."

Her niece smiled, and Alexandria swung out of the cart, calling in her awkward French, "*Pardon, Madame.*"

Her words stopped the tirade and the woman stared at her, eyes narrowed. Paxten also shot her a warning frown and then started toward her, his French too quick for her but his gestures unmistakable. He wanted her back in the cart and to stay out of this.

Folding her arms, she smiled, then said, "*Non!*"

That stopped him. He stared at her, blinking. Turning, Alexandria urged Diana out of the cart, then she leaned down and whispered a few words to her niece.

With his tone low to hide his English, Paxten muttered, "What are you doing?"

Alexandria replied in her halting French, "Getting us breakfast." She urged Diana forward and the girl approached the old woman, her French low and hesitant. The woman's suspicion softened a fraction.

"What did you tell her to say?" he asked.

Leaning close to him, Alexandria switched back to English. "She is explaining how you are returned yourself from the army because of a wound. And that you hate to talk about such things, but that you are a war hero."

The woman began to smile, showing crooked teeth. She grumbled something that seemed to be a question as to why did they not say so at once, and invited them into the Lafeu household.

Paxten glanced down at Alexandria. "How did you know such a trick would work with her?"

She tucked her arm into his. "I did not. But I understand

how it is easier to give charity than to be given it." She thought of all the dreadful pity that others had tried to shower on her for Paxten's leaving. When the whispers had wanted to make her into a broken, abandoned lover. And then after Bertram had died. She had learned very quickly to avoid those who seemed determined to make her into something tragic, for it only had ever fed her own wish to indulge self-pity, and she would not do that.

"Do you think," she asked, "that we could perhaps stay an hour or two to help her just a little in exchange for her hospitality—she might not want our coin, but she may take some assistance."

He frowned but lifted one shoulder. "Just remember, we could use some of that ourselves. And the longer we stay, the more time we give others to find us."

His concern did not touch her. She glanced at the bright sky, the sheltering trees around the farmhouse, the deep peace of the place. She thought of all that he had done to hide them—selling the horses, changing their clothing, keeping them from even so much as the sight of a city.

For once, she found herself able to be the flippant, carefree one. She gave him a grin, then said, her words light, "Nonsense. It would take an expert pack of hounds to follow our donkey cart! Now, come and see if Madame Lafeu can be talked into making an omelet."

Patience. Practice and patience. Drills had taught him that. And now Taliaris told himself again that those were the qualities a soldier needed. Was not this matter of stopping at every village and asking the same questions like a saber drill? So why did it not feel a task worth a man's time? Because this endless asking never gave him the answers he wanted? But going through the pattern of slashes and lunges honed precision.

This honed boredom, however.

If only someone else had been on duty that night, Taliaris thought, weary in the saddle, though he had had longer days under campaign marches. But then he thought of the letter from the general that had reached him this morning. General D'Aeth had been ordered to Santo Domingo by the First Consul himself to control that rebellious island. Taliaris knew what that meant. A long ocean voyage, and at the end of it an island in the Caribbean where death came more often from yellow fever than from any battle. D'Aeth had placed the redemption of Madame D'Aeth's honor into Taliaris's hands.

Taliaris straightened. That letter had been a good reminder of his duty.

At the sound of galloping hooves approaching, Taliaris reined in his mount. Lieutenant Paulin called for the column of twelve men to halt.

A horseman rounded a bend in the road, sunlight glinting off the brass buttons on his uniform cuffs. The man bent low over the saddle, his red dolman jacket flying behind him, and the plume on his shako bent with the wind. White sweat flecked his horse's dark-brown chest. Even before the man slid his mount to a halt, Taliaris could see the hard breathing of both rider and horse. Dust caked the man's face and streaked his blue hussar uniform.

With his mount fretting, its spirit stirred by the hard gallop, and on a tight rein, the man saluted, then said, breath ragged, "Sir . . . as you expected, the women . . . in the coach . . . they were not the English we seek."

Taliaris nodded. He had anticipated nothing else, but he had needed to check the innkeeper's story. There had been a possibility—a slim one—that the innkeeper had been paid to lie that the coach carried only his cousin and her daughters. It seemed, however, that a few threats had persuaded the man to give the truth.

"You detained everyone?" Taliaris asked.

The messenger nodded. "Yes, sir. As ordered."

"Good. We will see to them later." Taliaris frowned and

then glanced behind him. He had split his forces to send a detachment after the coach. They would return with less speed than this messenger. But then he had split his forces again to more thoroughly search for their quarry, and now he had men spread across the main roads in northern France.

They had also lost time going through that inn and the village. Eventually, however, Lieutenant Paulin ferreted out that the blacksmith had seen his neighbor, one Monsieur Degau, talking to a stranger. After that, to pull out the rest of the story from Degau, of how he had sold his horses and carriage, came easily.

This Marsett must have the devil's tongue, for he seemed to have not just the Englishwomen willingly with him. He seemed able to charm almost everyone he met. Degau, fearful as he was, kept repeating what a gentleman Marsett had seemed despite his unkempt dress. And how polite he had been.

Taliaris glanced at the dusty messenger and his tired horse, then nodded to his lieutenant. Paulin ordered the man to fall in. The soldier saluted again, then wheeled his horse and trotted to the end of the column.

Frowning, Taliaris scanned the horizon. Somewhere out there in the French countryside was Marsett. He could not have gone that far—not in a farmer's decrepit carriage.

They would find him.

Then Marsett would not only pay for his crimes. He would suffer also for causing them so much trouble!

Two days later, Taliaris found himself wishing again that he was back at the barracks in Paris for saber drills. The trail had seemed so promising, but now . . .

Taliaris glanced at Paulin, standing stiff before him in the temporary headquarters they had established in Clermont. Marsett had passed through here. And then—nothing. Taliaris frowned. "Two women and a man travel in a gig pulled by a

pair of farm horses—one brown, one a red roan. They must
be making for the coast, and yet they slip through our hands.
How is this so?"

Paulin shifted on his feet as if his boots had shrunk.
"Perhaps they make for Belgium or Germany?"

Taliaris picked up his wineglass and stared into the deep
burgundy. "Why? They are English, why would they not
think of home? That means the English Channel."

"Then perhaps they turned toward Le Havre?"

"We have men on that road. And to Calais, and to
Boulogne, and Dieppe!"

Putting down his wineglass, Taliaris shook his head. Then
he strode to the window, his hands folded behind his back.
In the yard, under a chestnut tree, a half dozen of his men
rested, sitting or standing, smoking pipes, drinking, sharing stories. When the next group returned from scouting,
these would go out. But to find what?

More useless drills!

Taliaris turned. "This Marsett. He must have guessed we
would find the farmer who sold him the gig. What would you
do if you wore his shoes?"

Paulin shrugged. "Buy faster horses."

"Or slower. Or different enough that everyone looks blank
when we ask. That must be it. We ask the wrong questions,
Paulin. We ask about a gig and farm horses!"

"But, sir, what else should we ask other than after a man
who might be injured, or . . ." Paulin let his words fade. His
captain had on a smile that left him uneasy. He did not understand his captain. But he did not care for that. He took
orders. He did his job. He was a good solider, and if he kept
at it, he would have a good retirement someday.

He straightened even more as Taliaris said, his tone brisk,
"Change the questions, Lieutenant. Ask after a girl with
golden hair and blue eyes—a beauty like that is not forgotten.
Ask after her and we shall find Marsett! Now go. And I want
answers by sunset!"

* * *

Two days and two nights on the road took their toll on his Andria. They had had to avoid a dusty troop of French infantry who seemed to be escorting cannons someplace—a sign Paxten took to mean that they neared the coast. With war declared again it seemed logical that troops would be moving to the borders, and marching out to stand between France and England. After glimpsing the uniforms, he kept to narrow tracks that had not so much as a milestone marker upon them.

The rain, however, broke his will to keep to the open countryside.

It started in the afternoon on the second day, a light mist that drizzled steadily. Not a cold winter downpour, but enough that only flowers and spring crops would enjoy it. Alexandria huddled under the blanket that Paxten had put over her shoulders, and even Diana's perpetual cheer diminished as the rain thickened.

Long before dark, Paxten found them a barn. A few coins persuaded the farmer who owned it to give them its use. But that did not put dry clothes on Alexandria. And even Paxten was tired of the cold bread and cheese they had been given as a parting gift by the dour, black-eyed Madame Lafeu. That, and potatoes stolen from a field, had filled their stomachs, but he had noticed that Alexandria only nibbled at their meal.

He could not blame her. With the smells of roasting meat coming from the farmhouse, this seemed poor fare.

Seeing nothing else to do, he made up a bed for them of sweet-smelling hay. At least it was dry. Then he persuaded Alexandria and Diana to strip from their wet outer garments and to wrap themselves in blankets. The ease with which Alexandria agreed showed how tired she was. But he could see that already in the deepening of the fine lines around her eyes, the pallor of her skin, and the sagging of her shoulders.

Diana, unwilling to rest, and with her blanket now worn like a Roman toga, amused herself with the barn cat. She seemed, Paxten had noticed, to have appointed herself her aunt's guardian. He had not been able to do more than kiss Alexandria's hand, or touch her as he handed her into or from the donkey cart, without the niece interrupting him. Even now the girl hovered close to her aunt. But it was not long until she, too, was yawning. And her eyelids drooped low.

The light of the lantern pooled around them as dusk fell. The quiet patter of rain against the stone walls of the barn, the soft shifting of the cows, the pleasant aroma of hay, and the warmth from the animals soon wove a lassitude that sank into Paxten's bones.

He sat with his back to the wall of the barn, the farmer's lantern nearby and flickering low.

Alexandria lay asleep on her hay bed, her deep, steady breathing that of someone exhausted. Her brown hair fanned around her on the rough blanket, touches of gold and silver glinting in the light, the mixture of strands tempting him to touch them. She had the other blanket wrapped tight around her, leaving one white shoulder, her shift having slipped down, to peek out from the thick brown wool. An enticing picture. But not one he could act upon. His mouth lifted. Two cows, three chickens, and Diana hardly made for the most seductive setting. Outside, rain pattered harder.

Would this have been their life if Alexandria had come with him nearly a decade earlier? He certainly had known lean times since then, and he had lived in worse conditions than this. What if she had brought her son with her? Traveling with Diana made things complicated enough. How much more trouble would a boy have added?

Perhaps it had been a good thing that she had not come with him. But such thoughts did not ease the ache and resentment in him. How different might it all have been if he had had her with him. For her, after all, he would have changed his life. She had cheated him out of that chance. And out of the life with her that he had wanted.

He glanced at Diana. The girl had fallen asleep with the

strand of twine that she had been using to tempt the kitten still in her fingers. She lay with her head pillowed on her arm. A pretty thing, that one. But much too much energy.

Then he glanced back to Alexandria.

She had woken, and now stared at him, the expression in her gray eyes unreadable. And then she asked, her voice wistful as a child's, "Do you think we might stop in the next town—just for one night?"

Ten

Instinct urged him to deny the possibility. Where some soldiers were, more would be, and that meant danger. To him, and to her and her niece. The danger increased as they neared the Channel, and they must be only a few days from the coast. Less perhaps. Or more if they got lost. Which they might if that gave him the time he needed to seduce her.

He smiled at himself then and gave up. His Andria might sit straight in the cart every day. She might eat cold food without complaint. And she might smile even when she rubbed what must be an aching neck. But while he wanted revenge on her, having her endure conditions that were hard enough when one was accustomed to them had not been in his plans.

"*Ma chère,* we shall stop at the next inn and dine like royalty and sleep on featherbeds."

Smiling, she closed her eyes. "I should settle for hot soup and a bath."

He promised himself she would have both. And he told himself that it was only to his advantage, anyway, to gain her trust and carve that path to her heart.

Then he shut his eyes and pretended to sleep as well.

The rain had stopped by morning, leaving the air fresh and the ground soft. Their still-damp clothes clung to them, but the sun rose warm in a sky dotted with white clouds as Paxten asked the farmer the direction of the nearest village.

Their luck held. Not only was it less than two miles, but a local fair was to start that day. Lodging might be difficult to come by, the farmer warned. But Paxten knew they would not be so memorable in a crowded fair town.

Diana seemed delighted by the treat of a fair. Alexandria merely tightened her smile another notch, and so Paxten put an arm around her and drew her close. That earned him a glower from the niece, which prickled along the back of his neck.

However, he put his attention on Alexandria, who had stiffened at his touch. "Remember, we have a pretense to keep up of being a married couple."

"I do not know any married couples who share embraces in public," Diana muttered, her tone as censorious as an old spinster's.

He glanced at the girl. "All you know are aristocrats who marry for land. The rest of the world is different, *ma fille.*"

And then he distracted her by telling of other fairs he had been to, watching jugglers and actors in Naples. And performing bears in Russia. And fortune-tellers in Spain.

The farmer's prediction proved correct. Even though they arrived before midday, they found only a single room for let, in an attic of the inn nearest to the town square, and therefore closest to the noise and bustle.

The room smelled musty, but a bed was a bed after all. And this one was wide and soft.

Catching Alexandria's eye, Paxten gave her a wink. She glanced at the landlord, then edged closer to Paxten. His pulse lifted. Was she thinking what he was—that there was more to do in a bed than sleep? Tugging on his arm, she pulled him a little away from Diana and the landlord. He followed, wishing the others anywhere but here.

She wet her lips, and anticipation hammered in him. *Yes, ask me. Ask me the question I already see in your eyes. Ask me if we can share a room, just the two of us tonight.*

And then she asked, "Do you need another of my brooches to pawn for money?"

For a moment he only stared at her.

Alexandria noted the shock in his eyes. His dark eyebrows

lowered and his lips parted as if she had offended him. Had she? But she did not think he would mind. Not Paxten. When had he ever paid any heed to matters of money? And then she remembered how he had said that he had changed. Had he really done so?

His mouth curved then, and amusement flickered in his brown eyes. "I think not. If there is a fair, there must also be a horse race, or a fight, or something else to gamble on."

She started to protest, then realized she did not have enough French to do so. He grinned at her, and she knew he was thinking the same thing about her lack of language skills. He turned away. With a few words to the landlord and an exchange of coin, they seemed to acquire the room for the night.

Alexandria glanced around the small room again with its slanting, low ceiling and its bare white walls. A few days ago she would have scorned its mean size, and she would have wondered how they could possibly be comfortable with a single bed and hardly enough room to turn about. Now this seemed almost luxury.

Then Paxten's hand slapped her backside, and she swung around to glare at him.

He said something in rapid French that she could not follow and tucked two of his coins into her bodice before she could pull away. His fingers brushed her skin, leaving behind a warm shiver.

"Buy yourself something pretty," he said, his French slow enough that even she could understand. With a nod to the landlord and a wink to Diana, he sauntered away.

Frowning after him, Alexandria turned aside, dug out the money, and then asked the landlord about a meal and the price of a bath.

The landlord insisted he had not the time or the staff to heat water to bathe—not with the fair on—so they had to settle for cleaning as best they could with sponges and basins in their room. Diana at least procured sufficient hot water to wash her hair. Alexandria contented herself with a good brushing and cleaning the stains from her dress.

They then took their time with their meal.

Diana ordered, and they ate in the common taproom, a room so crowded, they barely found seats tucked into the corner. Alexandria forgot the low company around them when the food arrived.

A plump, red-faced girl brought out spring-pea soup, gammon pie, roast mutton with a wine sauce, and a dessert of strawberry tarts. The wine could have used another year in the barrel, but Alexandria could find no fault with anything else. And the steaming dark tea and thick cream served put her into a charitable mood with the world.

Since Paxten still had not returned, they set out for a stroll around the town's main square.

Diana admired everything—the stone buildings, the cobblestone square, the ancient fountain in the center around which children played, the bright streamers hung for decorations from tree limbs and balconies. Everyone seemed to be in their best clothing, bright yellow scarves and vivid red waistcoats and pretty white muslin gowns. None of it compared with the fine silks and satins of Paris, but Alexandria found she did not mind as much as she once might have.

She stretched the rest of the coins far enough to buy her niece a wool shawl. She argued down the price by simply shaking her head over and over again. Finally, the woman added embroidery thread to embellish the cream shawl, and Alexandria agreed.

Time had slipped away from her, she realized then.

The crowd in the street had thickened. Daylight had ebbed. Music now flowed through the town, the fiddles loud and the tempo fast. Alexandria glanced about them, uneasy.

The lanterns hung from the trees and above doorways had been lit, and the sky darkened overhead to purple with the first scattering of stars glinting. Shadows rose deep and dark from the corners of the buildings and in the spaces where the flickering lanterns did not reach. Outside the inn, the landlord had set up a length of board across two barrels to sell wine, ale, and roast meats. Men stood about, slouch hats pushed back or their heads uncovered, colorful kerchiefs knotted around their necks, shirt sleeves rolled up. And they stared at Diana with a little too much admiration, Alexandria thought.

Then a complete stranger—a rough-faced fellow with a red nose—winked at her. Her cheeks warmed. Taking hold of Diana's hand, she retreated to their attic room. Diana protested, but Alexandria knew her duty—and that included keeping her niece safe from such low company and such increasingly raucous disorder.

Paxten returned not long after, smelling of ale and with his hair disheveled. From her seat on the bed near a lamp, with Diana's shawl in her lap and one corner now decorated with looping vines, Alexandria glanced up. Diana turned away from where she had been standing beside the deep-set window that overlooked the merriment below.

Frowning, Paxten glanced from one to the other. "What are you both doing here, when all the amusement is outside?"

Alexandria ignored the question. "Did you lose our money or win?"

"I lost—" he said, spreading his hands wide. As her expression tightened, he added with a grin, "Nothing."

"You wretch! But did you win?"

"Enough to celebrate. And why not? We have only a few days between us and freedom."

She started to say she would rather retire early, and then she glanced at Diana. Longing lay in her niece's eyes. But how could she sanction anything to do with that—that rabble?

"It is a bit crowded," she said, but the words sounded prim and not like the sensible reason they had seemed in her head.

Paxten waved away the objection. "No more so than any Paris salon."

She tried again. "Everyone sounds drunk."

"None as drunk as a lord. What is it? Can you not forget you are a lady and just enjoy being a woman for a night?"

That stung. He made it sound awful to have a seemly reserve.
Then Diana came and took her hand. "Please, Aunt. Could we
not just go down for a short while? For the dancing at least?"

She might have resisted one of them, but not both.

Perhaps she had been too sheltered. She had only been to for-
mal balls, and sedate musical evenings, and proper affairs. Any
May Day or fair she had attended had been with male escort
and servants to fetch for her, and the status of her position
wrapped around her.

A burst of laughter drifted to their room, and suddenly she
wanted to know what she was missing.

She stood, but with her palms damp and her insides
quivering. "Well, only for a short time, then."

Paxten smiled, as if he had known all along that she would
not hold out against him.

He ushered them out of the inn, and when they reached the
street he put an arm around each of them. Alexandria frowned
at this, but he only whispered to her, "I'm not dressed to have
you take my arm as if I were a gentleman."

She could almost wish they were dressed as ladies and a gentleman as they stepped into the noise and the crowd and the
smells of ale and torches burning and the musky aroma of
heated bodies. It really was not as crowded as a fashionable
Parisian salon. But in Paris, elegant society moved gracefully,
slowly. Here, laughing maids ran from grinning lads who
chased after them. Farmers danced bouncing jigs, whether they
stood close to the musicians or not, and careless of the tempo.
A few men staggered with tankards in their hands, singing or
simply grinning like fools. Women laughed loud and drank
back their ale as bold as any man.

It did have, she noticed, a certain uncivilized enthusiasm.

It also left her glad to have Paxten's arm around her. She had
not felt safe earlier, but with him she knew a sense of being pro-
tected. How had she come to rely on him for that in just a few
days? The question unsettled her.

But had she not always relied on someone? On her parents

to guide her, even to the point of selecting her husband. And then on Bertram. She had to own that he had known how to smooth the world for her. Or at least his title, position, and wealth had done so. What did she really know of anything beyond the small circle of society? Had that been part of her decision not to go with Paxten? Was he in part right—had Jules been an excuse? A way to avoid stepping into a frightening unknown?

Lowering to think that this might be so.

But possible. She had to admit that.

Still, she had brought Diana to France. That had been a step out of the usual. A bold step. And she had made it because she was so dreadfully bored with her life. Of course, she had come with her servants and her possessions and her title to make everything easy for them. Again. But all that was gone.

Fear shivered in her at the stark reality of the world that now lay before her. She almost turned to go back to the room.

However, Paxten shifted his arm from her waist and took her hand, speaking in slow, lazy French. "The dancing's started. The ale is good. And I've heard that a play begins in an hour or so. What is your pleasure, Madame and Mademoiselle Marsett?"

Diana bounced a little. "Oh, dancing, please. And then the play. And may I have some ale?"

Paxten grinned at the girl's rapid flow of requests. Of course she would want everything. But Alexandria pressed close to him and said nothing of her preferences. She had her chin up, and even in her peasant garb she looked too much like the bored aristocrat. However, he had felt the tremor in her fingertips, and he realized that she did not know what to make of this sort of entertainment.

He made a path for them through the press of bodies nearest the musicians, who sat under the spreading limbs of an ancient oak. He used a smile, a pleasant word, a touch to someone's shoulder to carve the way—the charm had always come easy to him. He had that from both his parents, he thought, for his mother had always been the most irresistible of creatures. And what he remembered of his father was of a man with an easy, quick smile.

Lanterns cast soft yellow pools of light around them. The moon had risen to add its glow, and while the evening held a chill, no one seemed to notice. Two fiddlers, a man with a hand drum, a flute player, and a dark-haired fellow with a guitar kept the music flowing. The dancers—mostly young people— kicked up the dust around the tree as they danced. Skirts flew high. Jackets and waistcoats came off. He knew it must look in-decent to Alexandria—she stared at it with those expressive eyebrows of hers lifted high.

It also looked marvelous fun.

"Come on," he said, tugging on Alexandria's hand.

She shook her head. "Dance with Diana. I shall stand here and watch."

Here meant next to three black-garbed old women, one grin-ning even though she had no teeth. He shrugged, and then asked the women if they would look after Alexandria for him. They smiled, then passed a rough wooden mug into his hand. He took a swallow of the frothy ale, then gave the mug to Alexandria.

"As you like, my dear," he told her in French. With a grin, he grabbed Diana's hand and whirled her into the dancing, and devil take it that it made his side ache.

Alexandria watched but too quickly lost track of them in the crowd. She stood there, mug in hand, the three old women smil-ing at her and urging her to sample the ale. She had nothing else to do, so she took a sip.

The froth left a bitter taste, but the ale went down with a nutty flavor. She took another sip. The ladies smiled, muttering French at her—something about her pretty daughter and handsome husband. She had not the words to correct their impression—nor the desire to do so—so she smiled back at them and drank more ale for an excuse not to speak.

As the music shifted to what sounded like a jig, her foot

began to tap. The old women grinned at her, and a jug passed from hand to hand, then tipped to fill her mug.

She tried to protest. *"Non. S'il vous plaît, non."* But the women answered in rapid French that left her baffled as they filled the mug to overflowing anyway.

She had to drink more of it then—just to keep it from spilling. It settled with a pleasant warmth.

She had half emptied the mug again when Paxten materialized from the crowd. She frowned at him but found it difficult to keep the expression in place. She would much rather smile. Still, she had a responsibility here, and so asked in her stuttering basic French, "Where is Diana?"

He gestured at the dancers, and Alexandria caught a glimpse of her niece, hair falling down her back in a golden cascade of curls as a tall, earnest-faced young man whirled her about by both hands.

She leaned closer to Paxten so that she could speak in English, for she doubted any but he would hear her given the noise. "Who is he? She has not been introduced!"

He took the mug from her, drained it, and handed it back with a wink to the grinning old woman. Then he turned to Alexandria, his hand out. "Stop worrying. Come and dance."

She hesitated, then put her hand into his outstretched one. "Are you certain you—"

"If you once mention my wound tonight, I shall run howling into the woods, leaving everyone to think you have driven me mad."

"I was going to ask if you are certain you wish to. Dance with me, that is."

He smiled, a slow smile that set his eyes glittering and quickened her pulse. "Oh, I wish it."

He put his hands on her waist then and spun her into the crowd. She clung to him, afraid that if she let go she would be lost amid the swirl of dancers. And then he spun her away and someone else caught her hand and turned her, and suddenly Paxten had her hands again. She only just managed to keep upright as she bounced along to the music, twirling from one partner to the next.

It was, in a sense, the same as any country dance, with changes of partners and two-hands-round and turns and steps. But it all happened so fast, with no stately grace, nor even a moment to pull in a breath. And all of it bouncing. All the dances she knew paused for flirtation and to allow dancers to watch other dancers. But this—she grinned suddenly—this left her giddy and her heart pounding.

As did Paxten every time he caught her, a smile curving his lips and those deep brown eyes darker than ever.

Oh, this was not a safe thing to do.

She lost track of time, of her niece, of everything except Paxten, who managed always to find her hand again.

The music ended with a flourish, leaving everyone red-faced and clapping and begging for more. Leaving Alexandria caught in Paxten's arms. She stared up at him, delight still dancing in her blood. Then he dipped his head to cover her mouth with his, a quick movement that left her no time to protest. Bone, muscle, and the will to resist melted in her. Just as the first time he had kissed her.

"I am going to kiss you, you know."

Alexandria looked up with alarm at the man dancing with her in the middle of Lady Amberleigh's ornate ballroom. The dance had only just begun. She had only just been introduced to him. Of course, he had stared at her throughout dinner, an unnerving, dark-eyed stare that had robbed her of her appetite even as it left her intrigued. She was not a woman at whom gentlemen stared. Nor was she the sort of married lady to be propositioned so casually.

Yet, was it a proposition? He spoke with absolute assurance, as if stating a fact such as that it had rained that day. And his voice, low and deep as thick velvet, brushed across her with just the faintest accent in his words. No, not so much an accent. More an inflection—French perhaps? Did his nationality account for why he would make such a provocative statement? No English gentleman would be so brazen. At least no English gentleman she knew.

She stared at him, a little shocked. And fascinated. She had never received much flattery before she wed. In the years since she had become Lady Sandal, she had become adept at the light flirtation required by society, but she had never been given such shameless words.

The movement of the country dance separated them, then brought them together. That gave her time to pull together a cool stare for him.

"You are very bold, sir."

He smiled, dark eyes lighting up in a way that notched her pulse up to a tempo far faster than the music. "And are you? Shall you kiss me back?"

She had no idea what to say to that, and she had to offer her hand for him to lead her down the two lines of dancers—gentlemen on one side, ladies on the other. Her throat dried. But she smiled and stepped through the figures. He squeezed her fingers before he let them go, and then allowed his gloved fingers to slide slowly away from hers, his stroking touch suggestive of other ways he wanted to caress her.

Face hot, she glared at him. "You are making sport of me."

"Not at all. I'm in love with you."

Her breath caught at that. He sounded as if he meant it. Startled, she gave a small laugh.

The dance parted them again, and again they met. His eyes had darkened. A lock of hair had fallen forward across his forehead. He wore his hair long, like one of those radical *sans culottes* who were making a revolution in France. In defiance of fashion, he also wore a plain dark-brown coat and pale breeches. No elaborate embroidery, not on his waistcoat, nor on his coat. No rings. No flashes of jewels from his buttons. Just raw masculine power under the satin cloth. And a lean face with a strong nose and a sensual mouth.

That mouth pulled down now. The dark eyes stared at her, intense, unnerving, beguiling. "Ah, but you wound me—it is you who makes light of my feelings."

She snapped open her fan to cool her face. They had reached the end of the set and had to stand out before rejoining the lines of dancers to go through the movements and up the lines again.

What did she answer to that? Did she beg his pardon? But he was the one saying such outrageous things. This was impossible. She could not dance with him.

As if he had seen her thoughts, he said, "Would you care to stroll in the garden instead of this?"

She almost said yes, but then she caught the gleam in his eye and remembered his words. He would kiss her. Where better, after all, than a garden to attempt to make good on such a scandalous promise?

"Thank you, but no. I doubt my husband would care over-much if I were to venture out with you." And what a lie that was! Bertram would not even notice.

He lifted one shoulder in a gesture she had seen on no other man—a careless shrug. He had been introduced to her as Mr. Paxten Marsett, a very English name and a very French one. Then he said, "And why should I care what your husband likes—you are my only concern."

He took her hand then, and she stared at him, astonished. A gentleman did not take a lady's hand. His thumb brushed across her palm, smoothing the kid glove against her skin. Her throat dried and she had to wet her lips.

"I want to do that," he said, stepping closer.

"Do what?" she asked, her mind suddenly empty.

He smiled. "I want to lick your lips."

Her face flamed and she tugged her hand free. "Mr. Marsett, that is enough!"

"Enough of what? Enough passion? Enough honesty? How can you have enough of those qualities in life?" He stepped closer, and she glanced around them, wishing they had to move back into the dance or that someone would rescue her.

But he did not touch her. He stood before her, so close that it appeared as if they were in deep, intimate conversation. "When I first saw you, do you know what I thought?"

She should not ask. But curiosity stirred. She lifted her chin. "What—that I should be an easy conquest for you?"

"I thought, there is a woman dying of boredom."

The absurdity of it struck her. Absurd, and accurate. She laughed. Others glanced at her, and she put her fingertips to her lips to stifle her amusement.

His eyes smiled down at her. "How long has it been since you laughed?"

She looked away.

"It's been too long, has it not?"

Desperate now, she glanced at him. "Please. I am a married woman. I cannot—"

"I don't care." He took her hand again. Tugging gently, he led her from the dance.

She let him. He had made her laugh and she wondered if he might do so again. Nervous, trying desperately to hold on to the appearance of composure, she followed him, guilt making her glance behind her. What would she do if he took her into the garden?

"I . . . I . . . ." she said, stumbling for a reasonable argument to make to him.

He smiled at her. "Finding more excuses?"

"I wish I could. You are outrageous!"

"So my relatives tell me."

And then, instead of taking her to the garden, he simply pulled her into a curtained alcove. One step, one tug on her hand, and he had her behind a blue velvet curtain. The fabric screened them, but panic tightened in her chest. Anyone could find them just by parting the thick drapery. Footsteps and voices drifted past on the other side.

She looked up at him, heart thudding and breath shallow. He could not possibly think of kissing her here. Could he?

He stood before her, slowly pulling white gloves from his

long, elegant fingers. He had wide palms and strong wrists. And then he took a fingertip and traced the line of her throat, down through the center hollow and then lower, to between her breasts. Heat pooled low inside her. Why had she not worn a necklace, or some lace, or something to stop this? But her longing betrayed her.

Please do not stop.

Closing her eyes, she let her head tilt back. An ache caught in her throat. Had anyone ever touched her so?

Voices drifted past the curtain and her eyes sprang open. *This is mad! I cannot do this. I do not even know him!* Her senses returned and she started to protest, but she made the mistake of looking into his eyes.

"Ma biche," he whispered to her. "I did warn you."

"But you cannot—not here. What if—"

His lips stopped her words. And the hunger in his open mouth loosed raw desire from her. She pulled in a breath. Then his arms were around her. He pressed her against the wall, his mouth hot on hers. She gave to him—gave because she could do nothing else. Because she wanted nothing else. Heat boiled inside her, melting thoughts and resistance.

Madness.

A part of her mind screamed the word.

And then she arched to him, and her hands clawed into his back. *Sweet, sweet madness.*

His mouth moved from her lips to her throat and she struggled to save herself—to save them both.

"You cannot . . . please." Was that last a plea for him to stop or to go on? "This is mad!"

He pulled away, his breathing ragged, his eyes dark beyond anything she had ever seen, and he took her face between his hands. "I can. To say I cannot is to say my heart cannot beat. Come—be mad with me! Or do you want to die knowing that you turned love away?"

Eleven

She had put her arms around him then. And she had kissed him.

She did so again now, as she had back then. Desperate for him. Her body stretched to breaking with need. She had, she realized now, never really believed such love possible. Yet, as his arms wrapped tightly around her in the swirling, loud fair—so unlike that sedate ballroom of a decade ago, and yet still an echo of it—she knew she had found something rare with him. He had fallen in love with her at once. However, had she ever said those words to him? Could she now? Did she dare?

His clever mouth and tongue teased away such thoughts, leaving her with only sensations. Fever swept into her, and the sweet ache for him. She gave in to the pleasure of it with a soft moan, and his arms closed around her, dragging her against him, pressing her hips to his, crushing her breasts to the broad, hard flatness of his chest.

And then Diana's bright voice, her French loud, interrupted. "Is the play not due to start soon?"

Paxten pulled away with an abrupt start, and it took Alexandria a moment to steady herself. Then she stared at Diana. The girl stood next to them, a forced smile in place. Alexandria glanced at Paxten. He seemed amused, and he looked not the least dazed by that kiss.

Putting a hand to her hair, she remembered that she had worn it down. She had no curls to tidy this time, unlike so many years earlier. Thoughts and feelings tumbled as if tossed loose into the ocean. She glanced at Paxten again. The man could turn her inside out, it seemed.

Is that what he wanted from her? To put her under his spell again. Did he love her still? Or was she now merely an amusement? Her head spun, and she knew she could not make sense of anything. But still she wondered. Was he still the man who had fallen so instantly, so passionately, in love with her?

Only how could he be after she had hurt him so deeply?

One thing remained clear to her. She would be a fool not to try now for that love he had once offered her. But the doubt nagged—what if he had changed from the man she had once loved into someone far different?

Inserting herself between them, Diana dragged them toward the other end of the square, where a makeshift stage had been raised. Half-dazed, Alexandria allowed it.

They sat on the ground. Paxten brought them wine, then left them to return in a few moments with apple tartlets and thick slices of soft cheese.

The food distracted Diana enough that Paxten had time to seat himself next to her aunt. Diana looked up to see him leaning close to her aunt, saying something—perhaps translating the play that had started.

Color bloomed in her aunt's cheeks, and her eyes sparkled. Diana frowned even more.

It would not do. No, it simply would not do for this Mr. Marsett to seduce her aunt in this shameless fashion—he had kissed Aunt Alexandria again, and had said not a word as to marriage! That alone showed him to be a rogue. Even worse, he had been involved with another woman only a few days before. And Aunt Alexandria seemed not even to recall such a thing.

Of course, that might be due to those kisses.

Diana scowled at him.

The play—a farce about the usual misunderstanding between lovers—did not improve her mood. Her aunt laughed aloud at several parts—due, Diana suspected, to Mr. Marsett whispering translations in her ear. Certainly he whispered something that had her aunt smiling at him as if infatuated.

She thought about pretending illness so that they must return to the inn. Only she had a disgustingly healthy constitution. And her aunt knew it. She tried yawning and pretending to be sleepy, but her aunt seemed so caught up with Mr. Marsett that she did not even notice.

Alarm tightened inside Diana.

She knew the signs—she had seen them often enough in Henrietta, who wore her heart for all to see. But she had thought her aunt past the years of folly—and beyond the age of losing her heart.

It must be a passing infatuation. Or the wine and the gaiety around them. Yes, that would account for it.

Forehead bunched tight, she glanced at Mr. Marsett, at his strong profile bent close to her aunt again. If only she had the reassurance that he would act the gentleman; that he had only honorable intentions. But she had caught him now twice with his arms around her aunt, and he had not said a word as to what he intended. What gentleman acted so callously? None she knew.

And there had been that awful scene she had witnessed between them, where they had sliced at each other like duelists with sabers. To bring them into an adventure was one thing, but she could not allow Mr. Marsett to drag her aunt into heartache.

Her determination to do something deepened.

Then, in the flickering torchlight that lit the stage, she glimpsed a flash of gold from a man who stood at the edge of the square, watching. She saw her chance. Turning to her aunt and Mr. Marsett, she whispered, her tone urgent, "Soldiers!"

Paxten stiffened and his hand instinctively moved to grip Alexandria's. He glanced in the direction that Diana had indicated and saw nothing more than men standing in shadows near the stage. Then the first act ended, applause rang out, and one man stepped from the shadows.

Gold braid glinted from a uniform. Paxten let out his breath.

"They have found us?" Alexandria asked, her voice barely audible over the clapping and whistles of the crowd.

He shook his head, the tension easing from him. "No. He's infantry, by the looks of him. Not cavalry."

This did not seem to reassure Alexandria. "Perhaps we ought to retire?" she suggested.

Paxten glanced at her. Then he nodded, and stood to help her and Diana to their feet. He saw them back to the inn, finding ways to slip easily through the crowd. But on the steps of the inn, he paused, then leaned closer to Alexandria. "Go on up. And you need not wait for me."

He had started to turn away, but she reached out and caught his sleeve. "Just what do you intend?"

He smiled at her and brushed a finger across her cheek. "Only to have a drink or two. Do not worry, *ma chère*."

Alexandria knew exactly what he intended, and she did not let go of his sleeve. "We spent the last few nights sleeping on the ground and the days driving in a donkey cart, and now you plan to go off drinking with the same soldiers we have been avoiding! Have you lost your reason?"

"Yes, years ago. And if I stand those brave fellows to enough ale, they will lose theirs and I might find out where they are posted and if there is any such thing as a port in the north of France that is not overrun by too many uniforms."

"This is not—"

"Woman, you argue too much!" With a smile, he pulled from her grip, then spun her so that she faced the inn. His hand slapped her rump, and she whirled around again, only to find that he had disappeared into the crowd.

For a moment, she thought of going after him. Then she remembered her niece. She would not abandon Diana here—nor trust that her niece might not follow.

Shaking her head, she took Diana's arm and started into the inn and up the stairs.

"I suppose one must admire his bravery, but he is rather reckless," Diana said when they stepped into their room.

Alexandria moved to strike a flint and light the single oil lamp. When she had the wick burning, she turned it low, then straightened. "*Reckless* rather implies that he gives no thought to his actions. I suspect he calculates them, actually, and then settles on the most dangerous course possible."

Diana sat down on the bed and picked at the partly embroidered shawl. "You sound as if you admire that trait—a little at least."

With a sigh, Alexandria sat on the bed next to her niece. "Admire? Yes, I suppose I do. There is something attractive about the notion of taking life in bold strides."

"But you do that."

Alexandria shook her head. "No, I am someone who thinks and plans, and then settles for prudence. Which has its own satisfaction, I suppose. But perhaps it can become too comfortable to always take the safe route."

"Well, do not start to tell me that you are dull! Father is dull, but not you."

Alexandria smiled at her. "Thank you, dear. But I am afraid I am, and I come by it rightly. Do you know, I do not think your grandmother, my mother, ever once raised her voice in her life. Never. She was the most terrifyingly perfect lady. She used to call her husband—your grandfather—Mr. Edgcot. Always. I never saw them so much as touch each other. And I must have been nine before I realized my father actually had a first name—some relative explained to me then that I had been named for him and that his Christian name was Alexander."

"Is that why you—why you allow Mr. Marsett to kiss you? Because you want to be bold?"

Alexandria shook her head. "No. If I were to be as bold as I'd like, I would—" She broke off, then smiled. "It is not that. It is just that, well . . . it is just that with him I cannot seem to help myself. He swept into my life once. And though I did my best to avoid him, fleeing to the countryside even, he still came after me. However, looking back upon it, I do not think I made it that difficult for him to find me."

Curling her feet up on the bed, Diana asked, "And then what did he do—after he found you?"

"Oh, he courted me. As if I were a girl and he . . . well, I had never known anything like it. Or like him. It did not matter to him that I had a husband, or a family, or that his own family disapproved of him. He was like . . . like facing a force of nature. One might resist, but eventually one had no choice. And I do not think I really wanted one."

She glanced at her niece. "He insisted when we met again that we must start over. So he wanted us to live the day backward." She smiled at the memory. They had started again with a kiss, and then dancing, and then dinner, and so on. She stared at the steady flame of the lamp, but her vision focused on other memories. "And then there was the time when he insisted we finish our croquet game in the rain. And the time he spent hours collecting wildflowers for me, only to have his horse eat them as he stood with his bouquet behind his back. And then that time in the upstairs picture gallery when he—"

She broke off that recollection, for she could hardly recount to her niece the full story of just what had gone on in the upstairs picture gallery.

She glanced at her niece. "He started to call me his Lady Scandal, and he teased that knowing him would teach me how to be as boldly scandalous as he. And then I heard that name floating about London when I returned. I have no idea how gossips seem to know everything, but they do find out."

"You care for him, don't you?" Diana asked.

Alexandria drew in a breath, then she nodded. "More so than I have for any man I have known."

"Do you love him? Does he love you still? Will you marry him?"

Rising, Alexandria kissed her niece on the forehead. She wished she had the answers. Instead, she had a hundred more questions herself. However, she smiled at her niece. "Dear one, I have learned one thing over the years, and that is that questions answer themselves if given enough time. For now we have a soft bed, and I say we make ourselves comfortable and leave Mr. Marsett to find his own way back."

Diana caught her aunt in a sudden fierce hug. "I do not want him to hurt you—you are too kind to be hurt!"

Smiling, Alexandria smoothed a hand down her niece's golden hair. "We hurt ourselves, darling. And a heart is never much good to anyone if it is kept in cold storage. Do try to remember that. It is too easy to think about protecting oneself, and we forget in the process how to live."

Paxten staggered back to the inn late enough that he wondered if he should even bother with sleep. The sun would be up soon. The dimming of the stars told him that. But he'd had enough of drink, and of loud laughter, and more than enough of swaggering boasts.

It had taken a few rounds to get those infantrymen talking. Then they insisted on returning the favor. After that, he could not get them to stop talking.

The First Consul, it seemed, looked to England as his next conquest. An obvious ambition given that Bonaparte had already had his struggles with the English fleet. Still, it surprised Paxten just how rapidly Bonaparte had been ready to move troops to the coast. But then, was that not the man's genius—to act when others stood undecided? Or perhaps to plan when others sought only to enjoy peacetime.

Tired of thinking about it, he climbed the stairs, one hand pressed to his side. Bonaparte, thank the saints, had nothing to do with him. And he had gotten what he needed—the information that most of the troops seemed to be headed to Boulogne. Which meant that it would be wise to make for Dieppe. Alexandria would probably argue with him over such plans.

He smiled at the thought as he let himself into the room. Then he paused in the doorway.

She had left the lamp lit for him, the wick turned so low that it gave off no more than the faintest glow. Coming into the room, he shut the door. He slipped off his shoes and then padded across the floor.

They made a picture as would stir any man's imagination— two lovely women in bed. Diana lay on her side, facing away from her aunt. Alexandria lay on her back, her face relaxed, one slim white arm laid over the covers.

He stared at them a moment, drink slowing his thoughts but doing nothing to blunt the wave of lust that rose in him. He hesitated only a moment as to where he would sleep. Then he moved to blow out the lamp. A gentleman would take one of the pillows and lie on the floor with noble sacrifice. But when had he ever done what was right? And he had his aching side to consider.

Feeling his way to Alexandria's side of the bed, he lay down next to her. Then he breathed in her scent and rubbed his lips across her cheek, the longing for her almost unbearable. Odd how she was the one woman with whom he had been able to sleep through the night. But, Mother in heaven, would he end up only sleeping with her and nothing else?

This revenge of his seemed to be taking a greater toll on him than it had on her so far.

Smiling at the joke of it all, he fell asleep. And into dreams of the past.

She lay in his arms, the winter sky brilliant over them and water lapping softly at the side of the barge. Pillows lay under them, and the remains of dinner littered the damask-covered table set in the bow. Behind them, behind the curtain of the open-topped canopy, the two boatmen he had hired steadily pulled at their oars. The curtains also screened the side of the barge as it cut through the dark water of the Thames.

Brushing his lips across her forehead, he murmured to her, "We could be in Venice, you know. On a gondola."

Alexandria's lips curved in a smile. She lay close enough that he felt her smile rather than saw it. "Could we now? And would it be perhaps warmer than a January night in England? Remind me next time you invite me to dine to bring a fur-lined cloak."

He grinned and pulled her closer into his hold. "Then why do we not dine next in Venice instead?"

She sat up a little and turned toward him. The moon had set, and he could see as little of her expression as she must see of his. His heart beat faster. He had not wanted to force this choice on her, but he had no option himself now. His cousin, the distinguished head of his family, had seen to that. He had to leave. Only he could not bear to go without her.

"What are you asking?" she said, her voice now serious.

He took her hand and began to stroke her fingers. "You know what. Come with me, Andria. A world awaits us."

"But I—"

He rushed on, interrupting her words before she could say no to him. "Bring your son if you like. Bring whatever or whomever, but come with me. I—"

He broke off. He had almost told her that he must go. But he would not use that with her. He wanted her to come with him because she wanted it. He stared at her, at the pale oval of her face. She had never once told him her feelings—never said if she loved him, or cared. But he had not needed that. Not so long as he could hold her in his arms and make her sigh and shiver and fall apart under his touch.

But he would not have that if he left without her. His hand tightened on hers. "Come with me. There is a ship bound for Naples that sails from London next week."

She turned away.

Sitting up, her took her face in his hands and turned her so that she had to look at him. "I love you, Andria. You're my treasure, my sleek doe! *Ma trésor. Ma biche.*"

He wanted to take her away with him—take her whether she willed it or not.

For her, he would break any rules. Society's. His own. For her, he would change his life. Once they fled the country, that dull husband of hers would have no choice but to divorce. And then they could marry. Yes, he would marry her.

But he did not want to face her with that. He might frighten her.

Please, he willed in his soul.

She looked up at him and then asked, her voice steady, but he could feel her breathing quicken, "Do you really want me that much?"

"Ah, more than that much. Tell me you will come! Tell me you love me! Promise me you will meet me and leave England with me!"

She took in a breath and turned to look at the dark water before them and the darker shoreline. Then she turned her face to him again. "I'll come. Where shall I meet you?"

He woke with a start, his throat tight and the betrayal almost smothering him. The feeling swamped him, bitter and sharp, as if she had vowed just last night to meet him and leave England with him. He threw an arm over his eyes.

Then he remembered that he lay in a bed in an attic room in the north of France. Sitting up, he glanced around him. He was alone.

Rubbing a hand across his eyes, he tried to put the dream away. Had it been a dream? Or a memory? He searched now for an answer.

He could recall the elation of the moment, the sense of victory that swept into him. The relief. He had kissed her and then had made plans with her. She had been oddly quiet afterward. He remembered that. But she had said she would come with him. She had promised.

But had she ever said those words he had wanted? Or had his mind put in those words, *I love you.*

Frowning, he rose. His mouth seemed filled with dry wool. And the ale sat heavy in him. His mouth lifted at one corner. He might want to wallow in the past, tearing it apart yet once again, but his body had its own demands, all of them centered in the moment.

He found a chamber pot under the bed and made use of it. Then he went outside to dunk his head in the fountain and wash the dreams and delusions from his mind.

Perhaps she had said that she loved him, perhaps not. However, while he could wash the ale from him, he could not rid himself of the bitterness she had left him. His fist clenched. He wanted peace again. He wanted the scar she had left on him eased. And he knew but one way to get that.

He would have those words from her. He would make her say them. And then he would laugh at her and walk away from her, as she had once turned away from him.

His mouth pulled down and he narrowed his eyes at the world around him. Perhaps this might not ease the ache in him, but he wanted her to die inside as he once had. He had loved her, but she had destroyed that. Still, he could burn for her. And he would. And she would burn again for him. He would make certain of that.

Ah, that damn soldier of General D'Aeth's ought to have taken better aim a few nights ago. The world would have been a safer place then for his Andria.

"But we are not that far from Boulogne. Why must we now turn for Dieppe?"

Paxten turned to glare at Diana. The protests had come from her, not from Alexandria, as he had expected. Before he could answer the girl, Alexandria did so, her tone mild. "Really now, Diana. He has already explained about the soldiers." Then she turned to him. "Paxten, when we do get back to London, do you think this is information the Foreign Office will want to know? I mean about French troops being sent to Boulogne?"

Paxten's mouth twisted. "I would be surprised if they did not know it already. Not all the English fishing boats in the Channel look for fish, you know."

She frowned. "And what will they think of a French boat headed to English waters?"

He gave a shrug. "They will think that it carries contraband—such as good French wine. But it will have us on board as well."

That answer seemed to content the ladies.

They slept that night beside the road. Oddly, neither lady complained. Not even when they had to make do with stale bread for breakfast. Paxten put it down to the fact that earlier a column of soldiers had ridden past them. Alexandria had sat utterly still, and Diana had gripped his arm, her eyes wide, but with a glimmer of excitement in the blue depths. He had watched, tense, but not worried. The soldiers, all marching on foot, looked bored, and he could not think that they had anything in their orders other than to keep marching.

Still, the next day, with clouds dulling the sky and threatening more rain, he picked his roads more carefully.

And in doing so he ended lost in the woods.

The flickering of a campfire in a clearing kept him from having to admit to anyone that he'd had no idea of their direction for most of the day. After following the narrow track toward the light, he realized his mistake in doing so only when he drew rein.

The firelight revealed a ragged camp with two shaggy ponies that had been unhitched from carts that were even more ramshackle than their own. Three dark-eyed, darkskinned children stared at him from beside the campfire, their clothes much mended and faded. An older woman sat tending a pot that hung over the flame. She did not look up at them.

"Who are they?" Diana asked, leaning closer to Paxten.

"Gypsies," he answered, guessing and glancing around the clearing again. Something did not seem right. The back of his neck tingled. And then he realized what seemed wrong— where were the men?

Picking up the reins, he started to turn the donkey cart in

the narrow lane, intending to gallop the beast away if he must. Before he could, two burly, dark-haired men stepped from the woods to grab the donkey's bridle, both older men, one with a jagged scar across his face. Paxten glanced behind them. Three more men—boys, really, but tall enough and broad enough in shoulder to mean trouble—stood behind the cart. He could not mistake the cold in their eyes or the glint of sliver that flashed in their hands.

Knives.

Merde, what trouble had he dragged his Andria into now?

Twelve

Alexandria felt the sudden tension in Paxten. She saw the thoughts turning in his eyes; she had her own. And she knew the look of men intent on violence. Five to one. Paxten would be on the ground and dead before he could do more than take a swing at one of these ruffians. She put her hand on his arm to keep him still. With her foot, she nudged her jewel box toward him and whispered, "Give these to them."

He frowned at her, then answered in soft English. "That's a sure way to end with our throats cut."

"Then, what—"

A querulous voice rose from beside the fire, pulling Alexandria's attention to the old woman who had risen and now stared at them. "You are English!"

She spoke the words like an accusation, in heavily accented English. Alexandria glanced from the old woman to the men with their hard faces and their narrow-eyed stares. They looked, she thought, like a pack of lean wolves.

Then she straightened, her heart beating hard and fast. She could see no reason to avoid the truth. "Yes, we are."

Beside her, Paxten muttered a curse. She glanced at him. "What choice do we have?"

The old woman's dry cackle filled the night. Calling out something to the men in guttural French, the woman came forward. Her black skirts swirled as she walked. Her silver-gray hair had been pulled up into a knot on her head. With the firelight behind her, she looked like a witch, her wide face lined by years and coarsened by weather and a hard life.

"You are wise, little one." She glanced at Paxten, then at Diana, and back to Alexandria, her dark eyes glittering in her heavily lined face. "Your family?"

"My niece," Alexandria said. She decided not to attempt an explanation for Paxten.

The old woman glanced at him, smiling now, but with a calculating look in her eyes. "You have not the look of the *Anglais*."

"I am *Anglais*. And I am not. I don't fit anywhere, actually."

She grinned, showing a gold tooth. "Ah, you are like us, then! Come. Share our fire. Maurice, bring our guests."

It sounded more an order than a request. The old woman turned and limped back to the fire. But the two older men, Alexandria noted, seemed disappointed. With a flash, the knives disappeared. She let out a soft breath.

Paxten did not look easy with the situation, and she could share his sentiments. But what else could they do other than obey? Only Diana seemed untroubled by the tensions that swirled around them. She stepped from the cart and bent down to talk to one of the children. The child stared at her, eyes enormous and solemn.

Glancing around him, Paxten eased from the cart, then helped Alexandria from it. The man with the scar led their donkey away to tether it next to the shaggy ponies, and two women, both of whom seemed younger than Diana, came out from the shadows of the trees. They stared at Diana, eyes wary. However, Diana chattered away in French to them, introducing herself, admiring the children, and soon the women came forward.

The old woman gestured for them to sit. Paxten did so, but with his back straight and his glance sliding around him often. However, it seemed to Alexandria as if these Gypsies had nothing to offer but hospitality now. Pewter plates were brought out, hot rabbit stew was served, and wine filled metal mugs were passed to them. Bread came out from a clay pot, where it had baked in the coals.

No one had much conversation. The Gypsies spoke little during the meal, and only to one another, talking in low French with so marked an accent that Alexandria could follow none of it. Alexandria could barely eat, let alone converse. And Paxten, too, remained tense and alert.

After the meal, the women cleaned up and the older man without the scarred face brought out a guitar that he began to tune. The other young men ignored Paxten and only occasionally glanced at Diana or Alexandria from eyes still veiled with suspicion.

Standing, Alexandria moved closer to the old woman, her curiosity unbearable. "Thank you for the meal. But why did it matter to you that we are English?"

The woman glanced at her, then smiled. "We lived once in the Vendée."

The name meant little to Alexandria other than as a name for a district in the west of France. But Paxten muttered a soft oath, and the old woman glanced at him. "I see you understand," she said. Then she spoke to one of the younger men in her own language.

With a sharp glint in his eyes, the man moved to one of the carts. He pulled out a leather bag that weighed his arm, and then spilled its contents onto the dirt.

Gold buttons glinted in the firelight.

The old woman grinned. "We go where the hunting is good these days." Still smiling, the old woman moved to help the young man gather up the buttons.

Alexandria stepped closer to Paxten. "Were those—"

"Buttons from uniforms. Yes. And these aren't Gypsies, as I thought."

She glanced around them, nervous again now.

Paxten's hand gripped hers. "Don't worry, *ma chère*. They're brigands, right enough. Bonaparte named them such, and aptly. But it's him and his army that they have no love for."

She edged closer to him. "But who are they?"

"In parts of France, including the Vendée, the Revolution never took, not with its hatred of both king and Church. The royalists there fought back. Then Bonaparte took power, so they fought him. Or they did until he sent his army against them."

"But why should they care if we are English?"

He smiled. "Because, *ma chère,* England most generously sent weapons to the Vendée. Not that it did these poor devils much good. I heard of families burned alive in their homes. Bonaparte wanted an example made in case others in France decided they disliked his being made First Consul for life."

She shivered, and then thought of the soldiers who followed them. Would they prove to be such ruthless men, led by the example of the general who had made the French Army victorious? She decided she did not want an opportunity to learn if they were.

Despite her uneasiness, Alexandria soon found little else to do other than to sit close to Paxten. With the guitar strumming softly and the fire warm on her face and hands, her eyelids began to droop. She yawned, and noted that Paxten sat straight as ever, watchful.

Then she realized that she had not seen Diana since their meal. Panic flared. She sat up, gripping Paxten's hand. "Where is Diana?"

An answer came to her from the darkness outside the circle of firelight. "I'm here, Aunt."

Then a black-haired girl with Diana's blue eyes stepped into the firelight.

Paxten straightened and stared at the girl.

With her golden hair and pale skin, she had been lovely. But with her curls now dyed black, and her skin turned a dusky hue, he decided she looked an exotic temptress. Her blue eyes startled by their contrast with the dark tresses. And how had she managed that copper tint to her skin?

He grinned at her. "*Magnifique!* But hardly a disguise that allows you to fade into insignificance. Perhaps, Andria, you should have allowed her the breeches of a boy after all."

Diana gave him a saucy look, but then Alexandria was on her feet and touching a hand to her niece's cheek. "What have you done to your skin?"

"It is only dye. Madeleine swears it will wear off in a few weeks."

"Weeks!"

Paxten decided he had best intervene. Alexandria's eyes had darkened and her brows pulled flat, and unless he missed his guess, she was about to give her niece a thundering scold.

He owed the girl no help. However, he had no heart to take the triumphant gleam from her eyes. Besides, she did look quite fetching, and they could use any help they could come by to keep themselves hidden. This made her no less stunning, but heaven help anyone now searching for a beautiful blond girl.

"*C'est bien,* Andria. Perhaps you should dye your skin as well. I think I would like you dusky as an exotic houri."

She glared at him. "Yes, I expect you would."

"And why not—I should like you in any form, *ma chère.*"

She glanced at him again but stepped away from him, as if she did not trust him. Or did not trust herself with him. He smiled at that. Then, with a resigned sigh, she looked again at her niece. "Well, I suppose it cannot be too awful if it will wear off."

Diana's new appearance seemed to amuse the Vendéans. As did Alexandria's reaction to her niece's transformation.

Paxten did not relax, however. The men might smile, but he did not trust that their mood might not shift. And so he lay with his back against a tree and his eyes open a slit as the moon rose and the fire died and the others settled to sleep.

The morning dawned with mist, and Paxten watched it rise, swirling thick through the camp. He had been lost before this. In such fog, how would he find the road to Dieppe?

Shaking his head, he turned to wake Diana and Alexandria.

By the time he had them alert, the Vendéans were building a fire to heat water for tea and coffee and to make bread. The men moved around quietly, their faces as expressionless as on the night before. The women chattered, however, in soft voices, talking to each other, waking their children.

He stepped closer to Alexandria, a hand pressed to his side, for the cold of the night had left him stiff and aching. "We should go soon. We have a way yet to the coast."

He spoke softly, and in English, but the old Vendéan woman still overheard him. She looked up from her seat by the fire, a steaming mug of tea in her hands. Her eyes glittered with speculation. "The coast? What—ah, now I see. You must be that half-Englishman the soldiers seek. The dangerous one who raped a Frenchwoman, is that not what they say?"

Paulin saw his comfortable retirement disappearing. He would be lucky not to end his days posted to the farthest colony possible for his failure.

He could swear they had caught the trail of that damned Marsett and those Englishwomen. They had been seen in a town during its spring fair. Only now all trace of them had vanished again. Did the man have a pact with the devil? Or had he, after that fair, raped and murdered the women and doubled back to Paris? Is that not how a desperate criminal ought to act?

Only no one acted as they should in this.

The captain had made this hunt an obsession. And this Marsett danced them across the countryside as if it were a game. Bah, why did they not just find someone who looked enough like Marsett and shoot him? Who would know, after all? And they could go back to Paris and to the real work of a soldier. France was at war again, was She not?

But that would not do for the captain, it seemed. No, he had to have this half-English cur even if it meant they must search for phantoms. Bah—they would become ruined men if this misadventure went any more sour.

The captain turned from the crossroad where he had been standing and strode back to Paulin. Paulin wiped away his thoughts as if they had not existed. Straightening, he kept his stare on the crossroad sign.

"Are they still making for Boulogne?"

Paulin risked a glance at the captain. He looked older than he had two weeks ago—much older. Fatigue lined his face and dulled his eyes. Paulin had no answer for a question that sounded almost a guess, so he asked, "Shall I order the men to mount?"

Boulogne, Dieppe, Calais—he did not care where they rode as long as they reached a port town and the end of this chase. He wanted new orders. Ones that had a chance of success.

The captain turned from him and stared at the road. Then he looked at Paulin, his eyes narrowed. "What would you do?"

Paulin considered offering the suggestion of murdering the women and going back to Paris, but the hard look in the captain's eyes kept him from speaking. He did not want to be thought a fool for making such a guess. So he shifted his weight. "I can't think like Marsett—he's English!"

The captain's mouth edged up. Paulin shifted his weight again, even more uncomfortable now.

"And that makes him different, does it?"

Paulin lifted one shoulder. "Who understands the English? Why does he go this way, then that, as if drunk? How can he disappear as if the devil had his hand over him?" *And why do we care?* Paulin added to himself.

"No, he's not drunk. And he may be the devil, but it's not black arts that aid him. He's smart, this one. He keeps to back roads. He finds ways to disguise himself. But it will not save him. I swear, it will not." He stared at Paulin. "Would you feel different about this, Lieutenant, if Marsett had had your sister, or your mother, instead of the general's wife?"

Paulin's mouth hardened.

The captain nodded. "Just so. Madame D'Aeth may be an-other man's wife, but she has been dishonored. We cannot let that go. Now—Boulogne? Dieppe? Or some fishing village between?"

Paulin frowned. "Not a village. Too hard to buy passage. And too easy to stand out as a stranger. He needs a town where another face is just another face. I'd want Boulogne. Or Calais. And a short crossing."

The captain nodded. "Yes. But they sent the coach to Calais as a ruse, so they would not take that road. Not if they hoped we would be on it. That leaves Boulogne and Dieppe—it must be one of them. So we will go to both."

"Sir?"

"Take half the men to Boulogne. Report to the commander and obtain what assistance you can to search the town, then question every captain of every boat. If Marsett is not there, remain until I send you word. I'll take the rest of the men to Dieppe."

Paulin's frown deepened. "But, sir . . ."

"You have some other thoughts, Lieutenant?"

Paulin did. However, he had his orders now. And at least they put an end in sight.

He straightened and then saluted. "No, sir!" Shouting out the names of the men who would ride with him, he turned away and swung up onto the back of his sturdy bay mare.

He glanced once more at the captain, standing in the road still, holding the reins to his brown gelding, the remaining nine men standing behind him. Gratitude flared in him that he did not have any such thing as honor that nipped at his heels like a hound.

"Good luck, sir!" he called, then spun his mount and set out at a canter. And he could almost pity this Marsett to have to face the captain now. After all the trouble the man had caused, he would be lucky if the captain allowed him to die quickly.

* * *

Paxten had braced himself, uncertain what the Vendéans would now think of him. He doubted they had any love for a French general, but many of them were devout Catholics. And they viewed themselves as patriots. Would they think him one too, or judge him a criminal?

The old woman grinned at him. "That whore of a general's wife got better than she deserved if she had you. But you had best travel with us if you wish to stay alive. We met two of the soldiers hunting you already."

Paxten thought of the gold buttons spilled into the dirt. Buttons from uniforms. And he tried to think of some reason why they could not travel together. But why should they not? The Vendéans knew the countryside better than he. And while they might be murderous when it came to the French Army, they had been hospitable enough so far.

He glanced at Alexandria's pale face and Diana's wide blue eyes and decided that perhaps there was a bargain he could strike with the old woman that might help keep them safe. And get them to Dieppe.

It took three days and two more cold nights on the ground to reach the cliffs over Dieppe. Paxten knew that he had lost his vigilance, but the Vendéans had shown them nothing but an indifferent kindness—as if he and Alexandria were sheep they took to market. Diana was a different matter.

She seemed to have become an adopted daughter. The children clutched her skirts, and when the group stopped to camp each night, the little ones dragged her into their games. The other young women braided her hair, and the men began to smile at her and flirt with her.

And that meant that Alexandria had not a look or moment to spare. She hovered next to Diana, as anxious as any mother.

Paxten found his feelings mixed as they gained the cliff tops and could look down at the curve of the port town of Dieppe with its narrow streets and tidy cottages. On the bluffs, windmills perched. A few houses stood on the slopes that led to the water. Across from them a headland jutted into the sea, creating a natural, wide cove.

In the distance, the choppy waters that lay between France and England stretched out. The time had come for a reckoning. Dieppe would be their last stop before England. And then what would happen between him and Alexandria?

The wind blew sharp on the cliff tops, flattening the grass and pressing Diana's and Alexandria's skirts against their legs. Paxten turned away from the view to go back and speak with the old woman.

As he did, he felt Alexandria's stare on him. But he had business yet to finish with the Vendéans.

Turning to watch Paxten, Alexandria shaded her eyes from the bright sunlight. Though she had not been able to follow all of Paxten's conversation with the woman, she knew he had struck some sort of bargain with her. What had he promised the woman to bring them to Dieppe? More of her jewels? It did not matter.

She turned her back to the land and lifted her face to the salt-tanged air. Home. England. Across the gray water lay safety and security. Or at least their illusions.

She pulled in a deep breath.

She wanted to spread her arms wide, as if she could fly. She felt that light, that soaring. Paxten could give away her jewels. And why not? Everything else had been stripped from her: her silken clothes, her satin shoes, her servants, her luggage, and all the things she had once used to make life pleasant. Everything that weighed her down.

She wanted them gone. All of them. They had been distractions, really, to keep her from noticing how little of value she really had.

Turning away from the ocean, she watched Paxten, admiring his broad shoulders and straight back. The wind tugged at his dark-brown hair and at his open waistcoat. She saw him gesture to Maximilian, their donkey, and their cart.

Something tugged at her heart. The words lay on her lips to tell him not to give that away. Give away the jewels instead, and they would climb back into the cart and stay on the road, vagabonds drifting with the wind. When had she ever felt more alive than over the past few days with him and Diana in that tiny, uncomfortable cart?

Then she glanced at her niece, who was hugging the children and brushing tears back, and giving her cream shawl to one of the Vendéan girls.

She had Diana to think of still. Diana had to go home, to the life that lay before her and the opportunities there. A boy ran forward to give Diana a daisy plucked from the roadside. Alexandria's throat tightened. She, too, had a son to whom she must return.

But what happened now to Paxten?

He must come with them to England, of course. But then what?

He turned away from the Vendéans and came to her, and suddenly she had to know.

"Paxten, what—"

Smiling, he put a finger across her lips, stopping her words. "Not now. Not here. We've a walk into Dieppe yet, and a boat to hire. And enough time yet."

She nodded and then linked her fingers through his.

Diana had to pause to say her farewells to Maximilian, and then they parted company with the Vendéans. Alexandria glanced back once, but the Vendéans had already vanished down the road, going their own way again, now the owners of a donkey and a new cart.

She thought again of the gold buttons they collected. Then she shook her head and started toward Dieppe.

The port town bustled. Fishermen mended nets on a rocky beach near the quay, sitting on their fishing boats, talking as they worked or mended canvas sails. Others called out the price for their morning catch, which had begun to give off a strong odor. Women hurried past them, baskets on their arms, their glances curious. Near the docks of the quay, rigging clanged, wood against wood, and ships groaned as if unhappy to be trapped at anchor. A few men stood around, idle, smoking long pipes or talking, their garb that of sailors with wide legs to their trousers.

Stares followed them as they walked. And Paxten decided that they must look as disreputable as Gypsies. Something had to be done about that. They stood out far too much. Not a good thing in a town that had its share of military men garrisoned here.

Twice he pulled Alexandria and Diana into narrow alleys, once to avoid a chattering, casual group of soldiers, then later as a double column of infantrymen marched past the quay. They left Paxten uneasy. However, he glimpsed no sight of a hussar uniform.

The first task was to find passage. For that, Paxten wanted Diana and Alexandria out of sight as he bargained. He wanted to draw the least attention possible, and Diana too easily pulled the stare of any man.

He found an inn—one small enough to be obscure—and dug out coins enough to buy refreshments for the ladies. Then he told them to wait for him. Alexandria looked ready with questions and arguments, so he kissed her and grinned as she smiled at him, and her niece glowered. Then he strode away.

He came back an hour later with coins in his pocket, more of Alexandria's jewels gone into a pawnshop, and what remained of the gems now promised to a fisherman who claimed to own the fastest boat in Dieppe. The fellow had a smug smile, but he also seemed to have a closed mouth—he had asked no question as to his passengers or their destination. He also had, Paxten had noted, crates on board his ship, and a glimpse into one showed champagne bottles packed with straw.

He grinned at that.

Since the man had goods already bound for the English coast, he would not mind making an even more profitable trip.

As Paxten rejoined Alexandria and her niece in the dark back parlor of the inn, he took her hand. "I'm sorry, Alexandria."

Her fingers seemed cold, and he wondered if that was due to the lack of a fire in the grate or nervousness. Still, she said, her tone teasing, "I should think so. To leave us waiting for so long."

"That could not be helped—but I am sorry that your jewels are gone. Or will be when we sail with the tide at the dawn."

"They do not matter. But do you—oh, bother, do you have enough that we might buy clean clothes and a bath, and a hot meal and beds? Those do matter, I find."

He grinned at her impatient tone. And then calculated the odds. Would they do better to retire back to the cliffs for the night? However, that would leave them too far from the quay and their predawn rendezvous. The fat fisherman had made it clear he would not wait long for them. Which meant they'd do best to present themselves now as respectable travelers, and be ready to leave before first light.

With that in mind, he took Alexandria and Diana with him.

He bought them all used clothes in a back alley from a woman who promised that the gowns had once belonged to a countess who had fled the Revolution. The gowns looked old-fashioned enough to date from a decade ago, but the gray satin matched Alexandria's eyes, and the lace at the cuffs and neck was a miracle from a nun's devoted hands.

Paxten bargained for the gowns, but Alexandria would not allow him to spend too little. The garments had once cost a fortune, and the old woman who now sold them ought to make some profit, she insisted. He did not argue with her.

He did, however, persuade the old woman into providing a room in which they could change. Straw bonnets and embroidered woolen shawls completed the ladies' outfits. Paxten bought himself breeches, a decent—if somewhat large—coat, a waistcoat, and a blue kerchief to wear around his neck. And, at the last minute, something else, a small portmanteau to carry their peasant clothes.

"Nothing so respectable as luggage," he whispered to Alexandria as they left.

At the inn nearest the harbor quay, he found them rooms, requesting baths for the ladies and a private parlor for dinner.

"Are you certain we dare?" Alexandria asked him. "It seems so extravagant."

He lifted one shoulder. Then he glanced at Diana and at Alexandria and asked, "We should be a good deal more obvious lurking about all day and most of the night. No, we hide in plain sight now. And hope our luck lasts."

At that, Alexandria's smile faltered.

A half hour later, however, as she sank into the hip bath, bending her knees to immerse herself to her neck, she decided this had to be worth any risk. Hot water had never felt so good. Then she began to scrub. When it was Diana's turn to bathe, Alexandria scrubbed her even harder, using lavender-scented soap, but the stain on the girl's skin barely faded.

"I do hope this is not permanent," she muttered.

Diana insisted it would fade, and managed to wash at least a little of the black from her hair.

After dressing again in her gray satin—in a room she had quite to herself—Alexandria came downstairs.

She found a gentleman in brown velvet waiting for her at the base of the stairs.

Pausing, one hand on the worn banister, she smiled and asked, "What have you done with the disreputable-looking Monsieur Marsett?"

Thirteen

Paxten smiled at her, the corner of his mouth barely lifting. "Ah, Madame Chantel, I thought we agreed that was not a name to recognize just now."

She came down the stairs in a mood to flirt, and the warmth in his eyes made her feel far lovelier than had the glance in the faded mirror upstairs. "Well then, Monsieur Chantel, allow me to say I ought to have thought of your dressing so fine sooner. If you had traveled as the Duke of Laval, it would have been so much more comfortable."

"But difficult considering the duke is twice my age, a military man, and would have needed a coach with a crest and a full escort."

She started to answer him. Before she could, Diana came down the stairs. She had put up her hair, and the cherry stripe in her gown suited her, but Alexandria still could not accustom herself to the inky blackness of her niece's curls. What would Frederick say when next he saw his daughter? And with that dusky skin?

Paxten, however, offered a compliment, and then ushered them into a small private parlor with whitewashed walls and a snug fire in the grate. A small round oak table had been set for their dinner, the china plain and the flatware serviceable—what indulgence it all seemed.

A question hovered on Alexandria's tongue as to if they could afford it, and she almost laughed at herself. She had once taken such things for granted.

The food could have been anything and she thought that she would have eaten it, but the inn served up delicate stuffed capons, sole poached in butter, and a variety of spring vegetables, including new potatoes and tender white asparagus with a mustard sauce. She ate as if she had been starved for days.

Diana ate even more.

"You'll soon fit that dress of yours, *ma fille,* if you keep on like that," Paxten said, teasing the girl. The striped dress did sag around the girl's waist and hips, Alexandria noted. But they had not had time for alterations.

Ignoring Paxten's remark, Diana leaned back in her chair. "The very first thing I shall do when I get home is to put on a dress that fits me—perfectly. And shoes. How does anyone bear wearing shoes that are not made to fit? What about you, Aunt? What shall you do?"

Alexandria stared at her niece for a moment, then glanced around her. "Should we not ask for dessert perhaps?"

They did. And for cards to amuse themselves after. Diana beat Paxten shamelessly at *vingt-et-un,* turning up twenty-one so many times in a row that Paxten swore she had stolen everyone's luck.

No one again raised the topic of England, but it haunted Alexandria.

What would she do? Would Paxten be with her? And would Diana ever go to bed and leave her alone with him?

With the candles burning low and the fire reduced to glowing embers, Alexandria decided that if she wished her questions answered tonight, she had best do something. She rose and took Diana's arm. "It is past time for bed for you."

"Oh, very well, I suppose we do have an early morning. Good night, Mr. Mar—Monsieur Chantel."

Alexandria placed a candleholder and lit candle into Diana's hand. At that, the girl's eyebrows rose. "You are not coming with me? However shall I manage—we've no maid." Taking Diana's shoulders, Alexandria led her into the hall.

"That has not troubled you any night before this. So I wish you pleasant dreams, dear."

Frowning, Diana glanced back into the parlor at Paxten. Then she leaned closer to whisper, "Really, Aunt Ali, I am not certain I should leave you alone with him. The man simply does not know how to hold himself within any bounds."

"No, he never has. And, quite frankly, I am tired of holding myself within them."

Blinking, Diana stared at her.

Alexandria smiled. "Now I have shocked you. Go to bed, dear. When you are nearly forty yourself, it will not seem so shocking. Besides, I only mean to talk to the man."

Reaching out, Diana grasped Alexandria's hand. "It is what *he* means that worries me. And I—oh, now I am going to start lecturing like Mother. Well, I will not do that." She gave her aunt a kiss on the cheek. "I shall trust that you know what you are about, for you always seem to. Good night."

Diana turned away, and Alexandria watched her for a moment, just to make certain her niece reached her room. Then she pulled in a breath, smoothed a hand down her stomach, and turned back to Paxten.

Did she know what she was about?

He stood by the fire, a glass of red wine in his fingers, one foot braced on the copper fender around the hearth. In his old-fashioned brown velvet coat and brown evening breeches, she could almost imagine that ten years had not passed. The white of his cravat, shirt, and stockings gleamed. He had such lovely muscular calves.

He looked up as she shut the door behind her and leaned against it. Then he asked, his mouth lifting, "Is your duenna put to bed?"

"She is—well, I think she believes you have dishonorable intentions toward me."

He put his glass on the table—which had been cleared earlier of everything but fruit, cheese, and wine—then he came across the room to her. "And what do you think?"

The glitter in his eyes left her breathless, but she answered, her tone almost even, "I think she is probably right. However, I assured her that I only wish to speak with you."

He shook his head, then asked, his words light but with bitterness underneath, "Talk? When we could do so much more? Where is your sense of adventure, Andria—or is it that you never had any?"

Her chin lifted. "Actually, I killed it when I had to let you go."

He stared at her and she pressed her lips tight. Heat scalded her face. Where had those harsh words come from? She had not meant to say any such thing. Nor had she wanted to sound even more caustic than he—but she had.

And then she knew the truth.

She had answered so because his words had wounded her. It did not matter if he had meant only a jest about her prosaic nature. He had touched the raw spot of her guilt for not having followed him. And she had lashed back.

She turned away. She had been stupid to think that they would ever be able to bridge the past. She had dug too great a ditch between them by how she had dealt with him—so why did it still surprise her when he sought retribution in small ways? Because she wanted to believe otherwise? Or because she wanted to think that what they had once felt for each other was stronger than this petty nipping at each other.

"Andria . . . ?"

She would not turn back to him, but his hands closed on her shoulders, turning her anyway. And then he said, his tone soft and teasing again, "I had forgotten what a delight you take in causing me pain."

This time she tried to take it as a joke. Swallowing the dryness in her throat, she looked up at him—and the pretense fell apart around her. "I don't delight in it—but you never leave me any other choice, do you?"

His smile twisted. "No—I don't. Do you leave me many choices?"

She smiled then, still aching inside. "No. I do not suppose that I do. Is that how we are matched these days? In our ability to scratch at each other?"

His fingers stroked her bare arms. Neither of them had thought to buy gloves today.

She glanced at his hands—the strong backs of them and the narrowing wrists. Then she looked into his face. His dark eyes no longer glittered, but she thought she saw regret mirrored there. And something else stirring.

"What will you do after we reach England?" she asked.

He let go of her, then gave a careless shrug. "Who knows. There is Ireland to see. Or the Americas—there's a rumor that France sold its territories there. Or perhaps I'll go east—I've not yet been as far as India."

She swallowed. "But not England. You will not stay?"

Paxten watched her, doing his best not to show his interest in her reactions. He had blundered tonight. He had meant it all to be smooth seduction, charm, and sweetness. Instead, he had blurted out hard truths.

Somehow he kept forgetting that he had plans for her. He kept tripping over his own pride and his tangled feelings.

Taking her hand again, he lifted one finger, then the next, and the next, playing with them. Her hand lay passive within his. Such slender fingers. So delicate. He did not look into those clear gray eyes.

"I was angry with you once, *ma chère,* for not coming with me, but that was so long ago. As to the future—well, shall we let it take care of itself tonight?"

He looked at her then, and watched the golden firelight warm her skin and draw soft shadows at the base of her throat and between her small high breasts.

Eyes wide, she nodded.

He leaned closer, close enough to see the flecks of green in her gray eyes, to see the edge of black around the rims, to see the faintest of freckles that had sprung up across her nose. Close enough to smell the tang of wine on her breath, and to breathe in the scent of lavender that clung to her now. Close enough to feel the heat stirring in her.

Reaching up, he tangled his hand into her hair, letting the strands wrap around his fingers. He pulled her head back as he stepped even closer, pressing himself against her and pressing her against the door. She did nothing but give to him, soft and pliant, her head angling back to expose her slender white throat.

You fool, she could love you again.

But had she ever really cared deeply for him? Certainly not enough to take the risk of leaving with him. Only enough to give him empty promises.

The bitterness rose like a poison. He ached to trust her. And still the voice whispered to him. *She made her choice—you know what she values, and it's not you.*

He searched her eyes for answers.

But he could not see what would be different in London now. His relatives would want him gone. Hers would look on him with scorn. And she would make a choice for re-spectability—she still had a son, after all, to consider. And she would not want a lover who would make her truly into Lady Scandal. He could see that in her.

His heart tightened, and so did his hand on her hair, then he murmured, the words barely more than a harsh, raspy whisper, "Why did you not come with me?"

Before she could answer, before she could tell him any more truths or lies, he kissed her. A touch of his lips to hers, as sweet as their love once had been—bittersweet now with memories of parting, of the empty ache for her, of what they had lost.

Letting go of her hair, he put his arms around her. Her hands crept up to touch his face, to stroke his cheek. She tilted her head and parted her lips.

Ah, he had what he wanted—her in his arms. His Lady Scandal.

Leaning away from her, he stared at her eyes. Liquid and

dark now. He searched her face for some hint that she would deny him tonight, that she would pull away.

She smiled then.

What was it he planned for her? To leave? To send her away? He could not think. Not with her smiling at him.

He ran his hand along her shoulder, pushing down the sleeve of her gown. She had such white skin. So perfectly pale. He kissed her shoulder, and she shivered with pleasure. His other hand found the ties at the back of her gown and pulled them loose so that the dress sagged.

How could he ever have enough of her?

His mouth found its own path to the shadows between her breasts, to the hollow of her throat, and his hands found their way under her satin and lace so that he could trace soft curves and tender skin.

Pulling in a deep breath, he smiled. "I could drink you up—as if you were wine. Deep, rich wine. *Ma chère. Ma bellotte.*"

She shuddered again under his touch. So soft. Warm, wet velvet. She turned liquid for him, and he smiled to know he could do this to her. When her lips parted in a soft moan, he covered her mouth with his.

God, she tasted better than wine. His senses swirled, and his blood raced faster, pounding through him with need for her.

With one hand he managed to loosen his cravat before it choked him, and then her clever fingers fumbled with the buttons of his waistcoat, popping them open and then tugging free his shirt. Her hands smoothed across his chest, her fingers splayed wide.

She paused then and pulled away, her breath as quick and shallow as his, and her fingers tracing the line of his bandage. "I had forgotten this—can you . . . ?"

With a chuckle he caught her hands and bore them down. "*Ma chère,* they would have had to hit lower than that."

Her lips curved in a smile, before his hands found her breasts. Her head fell back and her eyes closed.

He forgot everything then, except desire beating through

him in waves. His skin burned for her. For her touch. For the feel of her wrapped around him. Her fingers struggled again with his buttons, this time lower than on his shirt, and then she had him in her hands.

He moaned this time.

And the world became nothing but the sensation of her touch, and lightness, and soaring ecstasy.

"Not here," he muttered. *"Voici. . . ."*

He lost the rest of the words. With a low growl he pulled up her skirts and plunged into the heat he ached for. She arched to him, crying out softly, and that drove him harder, faster.

His throat dried, and his breath quickened.

Now, now, now.

Only he wanted that now to be forever. To go on and on with no stopping.

He no longer knew where his body stopped and hers began, only that her skin pressed hot against his and her body fit perfectly to him. As it always had.

She shuddered then, and her hands fisted on his jacket, pulling him closer to her, dragging him. He held out against her demands, but she arched again.

Sweet oblivion swept over him, racking him, taking him. Endless. Heart-stopping. Her cries mingled with his, impossible to tell them apart, and he kissed her again deeply, easing away from her only as his muscles loosened utterly.

Her lips seemed softer now—warm, wet velvet.

With a sigh, he rested his forehead against hers.

Her breath, so sweet and quick, brushed across the sweat on his face, cooling him.

His mouth lifted. "That is not what I planned." Pulling back from her, he stared into her eyes. "Stay with me. Lie with me. I want you in my arms tonight, my Lady Scandal."

For once, she did not stiffen at the name. Instead, she smiled—a small, contented smile. Lifting a hand, she brushed the hair from his forehead. *"Oui, s'il vous plaît."*

He tried to pull straight her dress and to button his

breeches. He gave up hope for any more propriety than that, but took her hand. "Your French is so utterly awful."

"I thought that a perfectly good 'yes, please.'" She followed him up the dark stairs without hesitation, lifting her skirt as he took her to his room at the top of the inn.

Moonlight streamed into his chamber from a small square window that overlooked the front of the inn and the Channel. The tang of salt air came in through the open window, stirring the lace curtains. Silver light fell across the floor and the wide, sagging bed. The room smelled of ocean, and of herbs used to keep the linens fresh and the wool blankets safe from moths.

He did not stop to strike a flint but pulled her into the room and shut the door. She had tugged her dress up over her shoulders, and so he tugged it down again, then pulled her into his arms. "Shall you cry *pax* with me tonight?"

She smiled—he felt her mouth lift as she brushed her lips across his cheek. "A *pax* . . . a peace? Can there ever really be peace between us?"

"Let us find out," he muttered, his lips already pressed to her throat. "Only this time without so much between us."

Burrowing deeper into the warmth of the man next to her, Alexandria smiled. His shirt now wrapped around her as well as him—they had not managed to rid themselves of all their garments. Her shift tangled around her middle, pulled low on her shoulders and the front ties now undone utterly.

Undone, as am I.

Lady Scandal indeed, she thought, her mind still drifting, and somehow unable to stop turning. Paxten snored. A light sound that both pleased and annoyed her—pleased, for she had so missed that sound, and annoyed, for it kept her awake.

She ought to sleep. She had not done so yet tonight. Only she wanted to rise and dance around the room, or to swim out in the cold, dark sea and let the waters hold her. Instead, she turned and told herself to sleep, to listen to the distant rhythm of the tides.

Paxten turned and gathered her to him.

"I thought you were asleep," she said.

"I am, *ma chère*. Asleep and having the most wonderful of dreams."

She bit her lower lip, then asked, "Is this only a dream for us?"

His arms tightened. "No, *ma chère*. This is real. Real and honest. More so than anything else between us."

She gave a sigh and wrapped her bare leg over his. "I do not want to lose you again—to lose this."

Propping himself on an elbow, he smoothed a hand over her hair. "Are you so certain? I am what my family would call a wastrel—and probably rightly so. I've no fortune, no lands, nothing to give you."

She brushed her fingertips across his lips. "Nothing but this."

Catching her hand, he held it still. "I've lied to you, *ma chère*. Lied to you and been ready to use you as badly as I felt you had once used me. This night—this was not meant to be like this. But I am caught in my own trap."

"What do you mean?"

He lay back, an arm thrown over his head. The moon had set, and in the dark room she saw him as a darker shadow, only the white of his billowing shirt visible.

"I—when I heard your husband had died, I did remember my promise to come back to you. That was not just my speaking of divorce—I lied about that to you. I wanted to punish you. For breaking your vow to me. I could not forgive you. That was really why I did not return."

"Oh, Paxten—"

His fingers pressed against her lips.

"No, don't tell me again how sorry you are. I don't want to hear that. I'm the one who ought to beg forgiveness. For that stupid anger. I robbed us of this as much as you did, if not more.

I should have come back—but I left it too late. Ah, *ma chère*, do you not see? It is not I who will leave you—not ever. But you will leave me again. Back in London, you will have your life waiting, and I have no place in it."

She parted her lips to protest, to deny this. A tight band wrapped around her chest, and her hands clenched on the bedding.

Is he right?

No, it could not be. She shook her head, but she tried to picture him in London with her and could not. Her throat tightened.

"But can we not—"

Heavy pounding interrupted her words this time.

Sitting up, she glanced to the window. The pounding had stopped, replaced by rapid French that now faded.

Paxten rolled out of bed, grabbing for his breeches in the darkness. He pulled them on, then swept the gray satin gown from the floor and thrust it at Alexandria. "Dress, quickly."

"What is it?" she asked, her voice hushed as she struggled into the gown.

"We do not want to stay to discover. Get Diana down the back stairs."

"I did not know there were any."

"Ah, why do you think I chose this inn. Hurry!"

The sharp tone told her all she needed—this boded no good for them. Opening the door, she hurried down the hall and let herself into Diana's room. She shook the girl's shoulder, then moved to find her niece's gown, which lay across the back of a chair, the white visible even in the gloom.

"Diana—do wake up."

Yawning, struggling upright, Diana muttered, "It is time to go?"

"Past time—hurry. Someone has just been pounding on the front door loud enough to wake everyone."

Pushing off her blankets, Diana pulled her gown on over

her head. "Really? Well, tallyho for us, then, I suppose. Do we go out the window with knotted sheets?"

Alexandria smiled. Thank heavens for the girl's bold spirit. "Only the back stairs, I'm afraid."

Paxten met them outside Diana's door. Voices drifted up the stairs, as did the loud thump of booted feet. Waving them ahead of him, Paxten hurried them to the back of the inn and to a narrow set of stairs meant for servants. Steep and wooden, the stairs creaked under their weight. Alexandria winced, but Paxten's hand at her back urged her faster. At least their bare feet made no sound.

Using the walls to guide her, Alexandria found her way down the stairs, and then they were in an empty kitchen. Coals lay banked in the fireplace, waiting for morning kindling to light a fire. She glanced behind her and saw only Paxten.

"Where is Diana?" she whispered.

A breathless voice replied, "I'm here. I had to go back for—"

"No time. *Vite, ma fille!*" Moving to the door, Paxten opened it, glanced out, and then again waved them ahead of him.

They stepped out into a dark alley, and Alexandria wrinkled her nose against the stench of refuse. Paxten glanced both ways and then started toward the glimmer of sea visible at their left.

Following him, Alexandria winced as she stubbed her toe on a loose cobblestone. Wet chilled her feet. She wished now for shoes. Her dress hung loose on her, and she struggled to pull the laces at the back tighter and to tie them. Diana had managed to get hers done, but her black hair streamed out behind her, tangled as a Gypsy child's.

At the end of the alley, Paxten hesitated. He looked up and down the street that fronted the inn, and then leaned closer to Alexandria. "No matter what, keep walking to the quay. We're to sail on the *Mouiller*."

Mouth dry, Alexandria nodded. Her legs seemed not to have any strength, as if they were now made from soggy pastry. And her body ached in odd places. Had it been only moments ago that she lay in Paxten's arms, satisfied and warm?

She shivered, the damp mist from the sea wrapping around her.

Paxten's hand rested on the small of her back, and he stepped into the street, urging her and Diana forward. They had taken only a few steps when the words thundered out.

"Arrêtez-les!"

Fourteen

Next to her, Paxten tensed. Then he whispered, "Run—now!" He shoved her forward and whirled, his shirt loose and billowing around him. Boot heels clattered on cobblestones, men shouted, and dark forms loomed in the shadowed night.

Alexandria glanced at Diana. "Run for the quay. Hurry!" The girl shook her head, as unwilling to leave as Alexandria. And then there was no further time to flee.

Paxten lunged at the first soldier to reach them. Alexandria choked back a cry, but Paxten grabbed hold of the man's musket with one hand, jerked hard, and caught the man a blow with his other arm. The soldier went down with a grunt, and Paxten swung the musket up and around like a club at the others.

He glanced at Alexandria again, then shouted in English, "Go on!"

Swallowing hard, Alexandria grabbed Diana's hand. Fear pounded in her, urging her to escape. She stood, trembling, heart thudding, Diana's cold hand gripped in her own.

More soldiers poured from the inn—a half-dozen of them at least. Light glinted off a raised musket. Letting go of Diana, Alexandria threw herself at Paxten, knocking him down as something rushed past them and the sharp echo of a report filled the night. A musket ball. A near miss. Too near.

Then someone had hold of her arms.

Struggling, she was dragged to her feet.

Two other soldiers had hold of Diana, and the rest crowded over Paxten, their muskets pointed at him as he lay on the cobblestones. The soldier whom Paxten had struck rose. With a snarl, he slammed a booted foot into Paxten's side.

Teeth and eyes clenched, Paxten rolled and clutched at his side.

Alexandria let out a cry and struggled to go to him. "Stop that—you, you ruffian!" She realized that she had spoken in English. They would not understand. She tugged on her arms, but strong hands held her. What was the French for *ruffian?* Or *to let go?*

Frustration welled in her, and she kicked at one man, her bare foot slapping against boot leather and doing nothing more.

Sharp words in French from someone—someone in command, it sounded—made her twist. In the darkness, she could see nothing more than another dark silhouette, this one taller than the others, with starlight glinting on gold braid.

Then the soldiers pulled Paxten to his feet and started to drag them all back to the inn.

Fear tight inside, Alexandria glanced at Paxten. He slumped between the two burly soldiers who held him, his steps stumbling. His shirt fluttered open, and she glimpsed the dark stain spreading across the white bandages. That vicious kick had started him bleeding again.

She twisted again, trying to free herself. And then rough hands pushed her into the inn. She tried to turn, to protest, but found herself thrust into the taproom. She staggered, and then she rubbed at her wrists and glanced around, her heart beating too fast and the sweat cold on her skin.

A lantern sat on the mantel above the unlit fireplace. The room had but one small window, set high. A moment later, two more soldiers pushed Diana into the room. The girl spun on her heel, then spat out a few words in French.

The soldiers grinned at her, then stood back.

Diana pulled in a breath, and Alexandria stiffened as the captain who had stopped them on the road strode into the room. Captain Taliaris, she remembered now. He said something to his men; they nodded and shut the door behind him.

Alexandria wet her lips, then asked in her basic French, "Where is our friend?"

He glanced from her to Diana, then strode forward. Reaching out, he touched a hand to Diana's black hair. She lifted her chin and glared at him.

Then he said, his English heavily accented, "No wonder we could not find *la belle mademoiselle*. Mademoiselle Edgcot, is it not? And you—" He turned toward Alexandria. "Lady Sandal? You pick a bad companion for traveling, milady."

Alexandria lifted her eyebrows, then replied, her tone icy, "How do you come by our names?" And then it flashed into her mind how he might have. Her hands clenched into fists. "Marie-Jeanne—what did you do to her?"

His mouth thinned. "Your maid? Do you think the army has also the methods Fouche's police once used in France? No, she and your footmen and coachman have been detained. After this, I see no reason to keep them any longer under arrest."

Alexandria stepped closer to Diana. "And what is to become of us? And . . . and our traveling companion?"

His eyes darkened. "Marsett? To recognize that cur is a little more easy than Mademoiselle here. But it is a pity the shot at him in Paris did not hit more accurate and save us all this trouble."

His stare traveled over them then, and awareness of her disheveled state washed over Alexandria. Her gown must be rumpled, and her bare toes showed from under her limp skirts. Her hair hung down in a tangle, and she had neither gloves nor shawl nor bonnet to make her respectable.

Diana looked no better.

Taliaris's frown deepened. "I must beg your pardon that we did not rescue you in time from this Marsett."

Incensed, Alexandria stiffened. "In time? Rescue! Do you imply, Captain Taliaris, that either my niece or my person has been compromised in some fashion? I shall have you know, sir, that our state of undress owes more to the

rude awakening by your men than to anything done by Mr.
Marsett. And as to rescue, I should call *this* abduction and
assault! Mr. Marsett has been a . . . well, not a complete
gentleman, but certainly I know him to be honorable, and
quite incapable of the crime for which he has been found
guilty without trial!"

Taliaris listened to her, his expression unmoved. "He will
be tried. And shot at dawn. And you will return to Paris under
escort."

With a curt bow, he turned and left.

Diana let out a gasp, then ran to the door. She pulled it
open only to stare into two rock-faced sentries, their muskets
resting at their sides.

Glaring at them, Diana said in stuttering French, "Stand
aside. I want to see Captain Taliaris."

They did not so much as glance at her. She thought about
trying to push between them, but they looked far too stocky
to be easily moved.

With a muffled curse, she slammed the door shut and
turned back to her aunt. Then she let out a breath. "What do
we do now?"

Her aunt moved to a wooden bench and sat down, then
rubbed her forehead. The poor dear looked exhausted, with
shadows under her eyes. Her hand shook slightly. "I do not
know. I do not know."

Diana frowned, then spun around and opened the door. "I
wish for a hairbrush, hot tea, hot water, and clean cloths for
washing our faces. And if one of you does not go to fetch
these at once, I shall start to scream and I will not stop until
they arrive."

Folding her arms, she waited. The guard on the left slid a
glance to the one on the right.

Diana's eyes narrowed. "You have until the count of three.
One . . ."

This time the guard on the right frowned at her. She did not
care. What would they do? Strike her? Shoot her? She doubted

that their captain—cruel as he seemed—would allow such utterly despicable behavior. He had, after all, stopped his men
from pillaging their luggage. Still, she risked a great deal. But
she could not just sit down and cry—she would do that later.

"Two . . ." she said, scowling to make her voice firm.

This time the guard on the left growled at her, "Get back
inside."

"I shall, once I have my tea, and hairbrush, and hot water,
and cloth. Three!" Pulling in a deep breath, she opened her
mouth. A thick-fingered, grubby hand slapped across it. She
drove her teeth into the fleshy fingers, the man yelped, and
she started to scream.

The shorter guard cursed her, the other lifted a hand as if to
slap her, and then the captain strode into the hall, demanding,
"What is this?"

The guard dropped his hand, and French flowed from the
man as he stammered an explanation. The captain gestured
for the guards to step aside, and as he loomed before her,
Diana paused in her scream. A tremor fluttered through her.

He did not look a happy man.

However, she was not pleased just now either. She put up
her chin and met his hard stare. "What sort of officers do you
have in France that you keep two gently bred ladies in a taproom without so much as an offer to see to our needs. I asked
for simple things—hot water, hot tea, and a hairbrush. And I
am treated as if I were no more than a maid at this inn who
can be ignored!"

The captain's mouth edged up at one corner, and he answered her in French. "I did not know English ladies could
scream like fishwives."

"I can assure you, I can scream much louder than that!"

His mouth edged up a little more, and admiration warmed
his eyes.

A treacherous softening eased into Diana, and she reminded herself that no matter how handsome he could be
when he smiled, he was the enemy.

He nodded at the shorter guard, and the man left. Then he turned back to Diana. "Is there anything else I may do for you?"

"Yes—give us our freedom, and allow Mr. Marsett to leave with us."

His smile vanished into a cold, hard face. "I cannot. Besides, such a devil is not worthy of your concern. But I give you my word that you and your aunt will not come to harm."

She bit her lower lip, and then she said, her voice low, "And how can I trust the word of a man who would shoot an innocent gentleman?"

He stiffened. "How is it that this Marsett can make everyone think he has such virtue. If you knew that—"

"What? That he stands accused of rape by a woman whose virtue I sincerely suspect?"

For a moment he said nothing, then he shook his head. "You're a child. You know nothing."

"And you are a fool! *You* know nothing!"

He glared at her, and she wondered if he would strike her. He looked as if he might. His eyes had darkened and his fists clenched. He leaned forward as if to intimidate her.

And then the guard hurried back with a wide-eyed maid who carried a wooden tray piled with Diana's requests. The captain stepped back; the maid bobbed a curtsy and then hurried into the room.

The guards would not allow the maid to linger but ushered her out. Diana thought of perhaps opening the door again and dashing the hot tea into the guards' faces. She and her aunt could escape then. But what of Mr. Marsett? They did not know where he was, and how could they leave him behind?

She settled, instead, for picking up the hairbrush and starting to brush her aunt's hair.

"Thank you, dear, but tea is all I want."

"Nonsense. We both need time to pull ourselves together, and then we can make a plan. We are practical Edgcots, after all, are we not?"

Alexandria looked up and gave a fragile smile. "Yes, dear—

we are. But Paxten is not. And now they are going to shoot him just because he is a rash, impulsive hothead! Oh, bother the man!"

He lay in a cellar. At least it smelled like a cellar. Musty. Damp. A vinegar odor of wine gone off filled the place. With a grimace, he lifted himself from the dirt floor. The guards had thrown him down the stairs. New aches lay over old ones now. The burning agony in his side, however, made the other pains seem as nothing.

Slowly, he climbed to his feet, then swayed. He could see nothing in the blackness, and for an instant the thought chilled him that he might be blind.

Then he grinned.

They'd probably shoot him soon enough, and so what did it matter if he could not see his execution?

With one hand out, he eased forward, the dirt cold on his bare feet. He found the damp, hard touch of a stone wall, and felt downward to the smooth edge of a wooden crate. The lid lifted as he tugged on it, so he pulled it open and put his hand inside. Straw crunched under and around his hand. And then his fingers closed over smooth glass and the narrow neck of a bottle.

Brandy, he hoped.

He pulled it out. But he had no means to pull the cork.

Exhausted, he closed the lid of the crate and sat on it.

He could crack the neck of the bottle against the wall, breaking it. But that sounded untidy. And he had no taste to drink stray bits of broken glass that might cut open his stomach. No, they would have to shoot him. Or hang him. But the longing to hold any hope for life still stirred in him.

He leaned against the wall.

Merde! He had been an *imbécile* to let down his guard. To think he could not be tracked here. They ought to have waited on the cliffs. Or anywhere else. But no, he had wanted his

Andria in a soft bed, and payment now for his desire was to have dragged her into the worst danger possible.

Would they think she had aided him?

Or perhaps accuse her of spying?

He frowned, and wished again for some means to open the bottle. He groped in the darkness for a nail.

As he did, wood creaked and light shafted down into the room. He stopped his search and squinted against the flare of brightness. Boots sounded against wood, and then a soldier loomed before him. An officer, to judge by the amount of gold braid that lined his chest. He wore the dolman jacket of a hussar, swung by a cord like a cape from his shoulders, the sleeves too tight to actually wear. And he wore the fitted breeches and boots of cavalry. Paxten knew the face. He had seen it once before—when he had stolen into Andria's carriage in that village just outside Paris.

The man certainly had the virtue of persistence, curse him.

Glancing up the stairs, Paxten saw another soldier at the top, a lantern in one hand and a musket in the other.

For an instant, he calculated the odds. Could he strike this officer with the bottle and be up the stairs before the other man could shout an alarm? Or shoot? He straightened, and pain flared up his side. He winced and knew he would be lucky to hobble up the stairs like an ancient.

He glanced at the man before him again—one of those young, square-jawed officers, stiff with honor and gold braid. He could not recall if he had ever heard the man's name, so he lounged back against the wall and asked in French, his tone intentionally insolent, "And what is it you want?"

"You've led us on a long chase, Marsett."

Paxten lifted the shoulder on his uninjured side. "I had no wish to lead you anywhere. I hoped that traveling with those two women would throw you off the scent. They did not want to help me. You may as well know that. I forced them to."

The fellow gave a snort. "With a gun to their heads, was it? I think not, Marsett."

"Ah, but I needed no gun. You see, I knew Lady Sandal years ago. It was easy to give her a story, and then, when she wanted to leave me, to send her carriage on without her. And to blackmail her into aiding me by saying I should ruin her if she did not agree."

"You're a liar, Marsett."

Paxten frowned. He sat up. "I tell you—Lady Sandal and Miss Edgcot knew nothing of my being a fugitive. They wanted only to go home to England, and I used them for my own purposes. They thought I had been injured in a duel. They should not be held to blame, nor made accountable for any of this."

"And did you forcibly darken the mademoiselle's hair to help hide you? And how did you coerce them into stopping in a town for a fair? As I said, you have led us many places, Marsett. I've heard much of your stops along the way."

Paxten's mouth pulled down. He glanced around the room, then at the bottle, heavy in his hand. Perhaps he should simply smack it against the fellow's thick head to get rid of any notion that Andria and Diana were willing participants in aiding an accused criminal.

He looked back at the officer. The man returned his regard, his stare giving away nothing.

One of those well-starched sorts who lived by his code of honor, Paxten decided, summing up the solid build and the clean-shaven face. Even in this dank gloom, the man's boots gleamed. He probably folded his clothes every night, said his prayers, and visited his family every Sunday that he could. And he probably viewed shooting a ragged half-English criminal as a service to France. Which it probably was.

But it ought not to touch Andria.

Paxten glared at the man. "Look, you can do with me as you will. I've certainly sins enough on my soul to merit harsh judgment—including the sin of stupidity where it comes to Lisette D'Aeth. But Andria—Lady Sandal—is an honest innocent in this."

"She did not look so innocent when we found you—after you had gotten done with her."

Paxten rose, jaw clenched, and his fist tight on the bottle neck. "By God, I ought to ram that insult down your throat! You preening, conceited cockerel!"

The light at the top of the stairs wavered, and Paxten glanced up to see that the sentry had set down the lantern and shouldered his musket. Paxten looked back at the officer, then his mouth twisted up. Might as well be shot now, calling this fellow to book for his remark about Andria.

The young officer, however, turned and said something to the sentry. The man lowered his weapon. Then the officer glanced back at Paxten. "Lady Sandal and Miss Edgcot are not your concern. I will see them safe to Paris."

"But not to England—sweet Mother of God, why not let them go? They're not going to make you a general for hauling in a pair of Englishwomen."

"No. But I might be made a major for shooting you." Turning, he strode away, but he paused at the base of the stairs and glanced back. "I can see now how you do it, how you convince others you're a gentleman. You must have been once. Before you became a rapist."

Then he left, going up the stairs two at a time. The light vanished behind the door and a bolt rammed home with a thud.

Swearing, Paxten threw the bottle against the wall. Glass shattered and the sweet smell of champagne filled the air. It gave no satisfaction. Sinking down on the crate, he buried his face in his hands.

He had not long to wait.

It seemed only minutes later that they came for him. Six burly fellows, three with muskets, one with a lantern, and two to drag him up the stairs. He let his weight sag. Let them think they had injured him more than they had. He had bled, but not so very much. And, yes, he ached, but what did that matter if he found a chance for freedom.

Only how could he leave Andria?

They dragged him out of the inn and onto the rocky shore near the quay. Not far from the inn. Why exert themselves any more over him, he thought, his mouth lifting a little.

He glanced around him.

The sun had not yet risen. Only the faintest lightening of the sky and the stirring breeze signaled that dawn hovered. Stars and moon had faded. The captain of the *Mouiller* would be waiting for them.

Paxten glanced at the quay, at the masts of the anchored ships bobbing softly as the tide turned, the rigging on them creaking. No one else in Dieppe stirred. Yet, Paxten thought he glimpsed movement on one of the ships.

He looked back at the soldiers before him.

One soldier dragged Paxten's hands behind him. Rough rope burned his wrists.

"Is that necessary?" he asked.

No one answered him, but another soldier pulled out a black scarf. "Blindfold?"

Paxten shook his head. The man shrugged but glanced at Paxten with begrudged respect. Paxten's mouth twisted up. Courage had nothing to do with this, but the mad desire for a means to escape did. Only he could not see one.

They would line up and they would shoot him. And Andria would be sent to Paris with her niece. He clenched the muscles in his arms as they pulled the ropes tight.

Then the soldiers paused and looked toward the inn.

Paxten followed their stares, and he pulled in a sharp breath as Alexandria and Diana stepped from the inn along with that hard-faced officer who had come to him in the cellar.

Mother in heaven, did the man intend to make Andria and her niece watch the execution?

Fifteen

Taliaris walked away from his interview with Marsett even more displeased than before he had begun. He could certainly see how the man persuaded others into assistance. Marsett had lied just now without a quiver, without hesitation. But the man had lied, it seemed, to make it seem as if Lady Sandal and Miss Edgcot knew nothing of his crimes.

Yet, Diana Edgcot had proven already with her words that she did know. And so had Lady Sandal.

Frowning, Taliaris strode into the small parlor he had commandeered for himself. Night still cloaked the world outside this snug parlor. Beyond the yellow glow of lamps and fire, the stars had begun to fade. He wanted only enough light for his men to see well enough to shoot Marsett. No man— not even the lowest of English scum—should die in darkness.

He frowned.

Why had the mademoiselle protested Marsett's innocence? Marsett certainly had not.

Odd, that. Taliaris thought of the guilty faces he had seen before this. Human nature existed even in the discipline of the army; men found ways to cheat, lie, steal, and murder no matter what. But the ones he had known always seemed to have excuses ready for their crimes along with pleading their lack of guilt.

So why had she called him innocent when the man himself would not?

That question—and his own curiosity about Marsett—had

driven him to go and meet that half-English dog. He had found much of what he had expected—a now-ragged man with the marks of dissipation on his face. A man with some charm about him, and with even features that a woman might find attractive. A man with an aristocratic look to him, with a strong nose and languid manners.

He frowned. Well, he knew at least that Madame D'Aeth had been assaulted. And Marsett had been shot as he fled her rooms. Those were facts a man could trust.

A knock sounded on the door. Taliaris turned from the window as one of his men entered and saluted. He recognized Melun as one of the two he had ordered to guard Lady Sandal and Miss Edgcot. He could guess what came next, but still he asked, "What does she want now?"

Melun frowned, as if he disapproved. "To speak with you, sir. That is, sir, Lady Sandal would like to speak with you. The girl asked us to find you and tell you."

Taliaris strode out the door but then stopped and asked, "How did she get you to move this time?"

For a moment, Melun struggled as if embarrassed by what he must say. Then he admitted, "The poker, sir." Taliaris raised his eyebrows and Melun rushed on. "She threatened to take the poker to every breakable in the room, and then to us. That one needs a whip taken to her, I tell you!"

Taliaris glanced at the man, his eyes hard. "How brave you'd look whipping a girl such as that. Don't be a fool, Melun. I've no doubt she asked nicely enough the first time for you to fetch me."

The man snapped to attention. "Sir, I did not think the captain ought to be disturbed by the likes of—"

"Melun. Think less and follow orders more. And remember that Lady Sandal and her niece are to be treated with respect and care. Do you understand?"

He spoke softly, but Melun swallowed hard and nodded vigorously.

Striding past the man, Taliaris made for the taproom. The

other man—Toulan—saluted, then opened the door for him and closed it behind him.

He did not find Diana Edgcot brandishing a poker. That instrument lay beside the empty hearth. But he wished he had seen her threatening Melun with it. She must have looked like one of the heroines of the Revolution.

Miss Edgcot and Lady Sandal sat next to each other on a wooden bench, sipping tea from china cups, their hair brushed and pulled into simple chignons. They looked utterly respectable. Except their dresses looked a style from the last century, and their bare feet showed from under their skirts.

His stare lingered longer than it should on Miss Edgcot's well-shaped feet: She had small toes, he noticed, and delicate high arches.

Warm now, he looked up at once and gave the women a short bow, then asked in English, "You wished to see me?"

Lady Sandal put down her teacup on a side table and rose. Her gown now lay smoothed and tightly laced. With her hair up instead of loose and wild, she looked a formidable matron. But he kept seeing her as she had been on the quay—pale, hair loose, and looking ready to fight like a Paris harlot out to defend her evening's conquest. He frowned at her.

"Captain Taliaris, I have a request of you. You have given your word already to see to our well-being."

His eyes narrowed with suspicion. These two had something planned. He knew it. "I cannot release you."

"I have not asked for that. What I wish for are a few moments with Mr. Marsett, to say good-bye."

Taliaris began to shake his head, but as he did the girl rose and came to him. "Please, Captain. If my aunt and I are truly your concern, then you cannot deny this request."

He looked from one woman to the other.

Alexandria tried to calm the nervous flutter in her stomach with a gulp of air. This had to work. It must. She had seen the attraction between Captain Taliaris and Diana—what young man of his age did not look at Diana with that dazzled expression? However, this young man seemed made of harder materials than most. But she had worked this out with Diana. Now she would have to trust her niece's skills.

Diana stared up at the man, her eyes imploring. She touched her hand to his sleeve. "My aunt has known Mr. Marsett for a number of years, and has been in love with him—"

"Please, Diana, that is saying too much." Alexandria said the words, then wondered if they came out too rehearsed. They had plotted this part as well. She would demur—and hope to heavens that the captain did not have such an insensitive nature that he responded by shrugging and turning away.

"No, Aunt Alexandria, the captain should know," Diana insisted, playing her part with passion.

The captain frowned. "Know what?"

"My aunt never had the chance to tell Mr. Marsett of her feelings. And if she is denied that now—well, sir, I fear it is possible that it might put her into a decline that could well end her life."

Alexandria tried to look pitiful. She knew she must have the pale skin for it, for her skin seemed cold as the barren hearth. And she had the frightened eyes—she did not have to act the anxiety that twisted inside her. "Please, Diana. We have made our request. If the captain cannot see to allowing me this small favor. . . ."

She allowed the words to fade, and she turned away. What would she do if he denied her this? She had to see Paxten. What if even now they prepared to shoot him? Her skin chilled even more. Oh, what if she heard the shots echo and knew then that she would never hold him. Never have his hand touch her face again. Never hear his voice call her name.

Something thick lodged in her throat.

I never told him I loved him.

She shut her eyes. A tear slid down her cheek. She dashed it away, and then realized that she ought to have used it.

She looked back at the captain.

He stared at her for a moment, and then glanced down at

Diana again as the girl stepped closer to him. "I would be deeply in your debt if you could do this. For my aunt. For me."

Diana looked up at the captain, her lips parted. She willed him to believe her. She put on what she hoped might be her most seductive gaze—and then an odd thing happened.

As she stared at him, he gazed back, his brown eyes open and searching. Shame for her deception warmed her cheeks, but she could not look away. She dared not. Too much depended on luring him in. She struggled to maintain her arch look, and then it seemed not to matter.

He had the most amazing eyes. Deep brown. A true, solid brown. Like dark tea. She stared at him, her knees loosening and her breath quickening. She wanted—what did she want? She could not think with him staring at her in that fashion. As if no one else existed in the world. As if nothing but thoughts of her filled his mind.

He leaned closer.

He had thick, dark lashes. Long lashes that curled slightly. And dark eyebrows, expressive ones that quirked or flattened with his moods. They lifted just now with the faintest inquiry, as if he wondered if she would protest a kiss.

Her pulse quickened. Would he dare to kiss her in front of her aunt?

A moment later, the look vanished. He straightened, pulling back from her.

She put her shoulders back and blinked. Disappointment burned hot in her chest. She looked away and told herself not to be silly. *It's only your pride he's hurt.* She wanted him to find her irresistible only for the sake of the plan. Didn't she?

She frowned at herself. Of all the absurd things—to be infatuated by a pair of brown eyes as if she were a country girl with no experience of the world!

Well, she was not, and she would not be!

So why did this ache well in her?

All brusque tone now, the captain turned to Alexandria. "If

this is some way you use to gain your freedom and his, I warn that it is my duty to bring justice to him. No matter what."

Desperation filled Alexandria. "I swear to you, sir, on my honor and on my son's life, I do wish to speak to Mr. Marsett. I must. Please?"

His scowl deepened. "Do I have your promise as well that you will not attempt escape—that you do nothing more to attempt to liberate Marsett?"

Alexandria drew herself up. "Captain, you know that would be foolish. And I have my niece to consider. I vow to you, I would do all possible to keep her safe from danger."

He nodded. The uneasy look did not leave his eyes, but he stepped back and opened the door for them.

Alexandria hurried forward before he could change his mind. And she prayed that it would not occur to him until later that she had not actually promised not to attempt escape.

With Diana a step behind her, she hurried into the chill predawn air. Clutching her arms, she shivered and wished for stockings and shoes and a warm wrap. The sight of Paxten drove out such trifling concerns.

He stood ten or fifteen yards from the inn, his ragged figure easily recognized against all the stiff uniforms. His shirt hung open, showing the bandage around his chest, now stained and dirty. He seemed to have his arms behind him.

She hurried toward him, and then her steps slowed as she neared. Her heart twisted. A new bruise—purple and swelling—marred his cheek. A cut ran diagonally across his chin under the shadow of his beard. Other bruises, barely visible under his tattered shirt, marked his shoulder. And his hands seemed to be tied.

Throat tight, she ached to reach out and soothe each cut and to pull loose those wretched ropes.

She looked up and met his stare.

He scowled at her as if he did not want her here.

Of course he would not.

Turning, she clutched at Diana as if for support.

"You must be brave now, Aunt," Diana said.

Alexandria glanced at her niece and saw in the girl's eyes that she was ready to carry on with the rest of their plan. Her mouth lifted faintly. Had not Paxten said that he always seemed to give her so few choices? This seemed the only one now.

She gave Diana's hand a squeeze, then let go and came closer to Paxten. She glanced then at the soldiers around him. "Your captain said I might have a word in private with Mr. Marsett."

They stared at her. Oh, why could not these Frenchmen speak at least a little English!

Captain Taliaris said something to them, his French so fast that Alexandria understood none of it, and the soldiers moved away.

She glanced at Paxten. "We do not have long."

He smiled. "I wish I could hold you, but they've tied my hands."

Her expression tensed, and Paxten wished he had not said anything. "Ah, *ma chère,* go back to the inn and close your ears and forget you ever knew me."

She shook her head. "I cannot. But I—" She stepped closer, and then whispered, her tone urgent, "The boat we were to take, it must be in view. And I thought, well, with your daring and my planning, we must be able to make our escape. Diana is ready for anything, you know."

Frowning, he stepped back from her. "Go. There is nothing more to be done. It's too dangerous for you to even be here now."

She glanced over her shoulder. Diana stood between the captain and her and Paxten, and she hoped their words would not carry on the breeze that now came in from the sea. She looked back at Paxten. "How can you ask that of me?"

"I can ask because I love you enough at last to let you go from my life. I did not have that before. Before, with me, it was all my wanting. It was, God help me, pride and lust. And I hated that another man had you."

He looked away. The sea breeze lifted a lock of his dark hair, fluttering it. Then he looked back at her, his dark eyes bright, and he smiled. "Ah, *ma chère,* I probably would not have been a good husband anyway. Let us end with the memory of last night between us. That at least was good. That was love."

Her vision blurred. "I love you, Paxten. I always have."

"Ah, *ma chère,* don't make this harder for us."

"Hard? This is not hard. Hard is to be without you. Hard is to wake in the morning without you there. Hard is to not feel your warmth. Not to be able to press my head to your chest and hear your heart beating. Hard is to never again argue with you, or never hear you laugh. That's all impossibly hard."

"No, *ma chère.* You have done it before. You can do it again. You have a good life."

"And I want a better one—with you. But if you will not at least attempt to go with me, then I shall stay."

He frowned then. "Stay? What do you mean?"

She linked her arm through his. "I mean just that. I shall stay with you—no matter what."

"No. Do not be silly. You cannot." He turned then and called out to the captain. "We are done. Please, take her back inside. She should not have to see this."

Alexandria tightened her hold on him. The wetness brimmed over her eyes, but the fear faded. As did the regret. "We found each other again last night, Paxten. I shall not let go of that. Nor of you."

She glanced then at Captain Taliaris. He stood still a moment, then gestured for his men to advance. Alexandria stiffened and looked at Diana, then said, "He will not go with us. It is over, it seems. My dear, I never meant to drag you into this."

Diana's forehead tightened. She glanced at the soldiers, then her lips thinned. She shook her head, then said, her voice only a little high and tense, "Nonsense. This is quite the best adventure of my life. And it is my privilege to be with you. And to do all I can for you."

She turned then and took the poker out from under her skirts, where she had hidden it. She brandished the length of iron before her like a sword, shouting, "Well, come on. Let's see which of you has courage enough to take on an Englishwoman!"

Paxten swore. He glanced down at Alexandria, and then at the captain, who now strode toward them. And he gave up.

With a twist of his arms, Paxten freed himself from the ropes. His tensed muscles earlier had forced a looser knot—an old trick he had learned from a magician in Genoa, and one that still worked. Then he pushed Alexandria toward the docks. "Go. This time, please God, go!"

She staggered a step and then stopped again.

Paxten swore. Taliaris shouted to his men and three charged forward. Diana swung at one soldier while another grabbed her around the waist from behind, lifting her from her feet. And then two more grabbed Alexandria.

Red heat flared in Paxten.

He slammed a fist into one man's windpipe, and the fellow went down gasping. The other let go of Alexandria and turned on Paxten with a grin. "Eh, come on, you half-English—"

The rest of the man's curse ended in a grunt as Paxten's knee connected with soft groin muscles. Red-faced, the man crumpled. Paxten looked up to see muskets trained on him, but Taliaris shouted, "Hold fire! Hold until you pull the women out."

Alexandria glanced at Paxten. "You see, I am of some use."

He swore, then slammed a fist into the kidneys of the man holding Diana. The soldier dropped her and swung around, teeth bared. Diana's poker caught him on the back of the knees, dropping him.

Crouching into a fighting stance, Paxten turned again. Six men had dropped their muskets and now closed on them. Not good odds. Not even when he had been in his prime.

He glanced at Diana, standing over the fallen soldiers like a modern-day Boadicea, then at Alexandria, pale-faced next to him but looking determined to keep herself between him and harm.

How had it ever come to this?

Desperate, he looked to Taliaris. There had to be some

other way to resolve this—to get Alexandria and Diana out without their being harmed.

His hopes dropped at the clatter of steel horseshoes on cobblestones. Two columns of cavalry galloped down to the dock, coming out of the predawn stillness like devils out of hell's gates. Dropping his hands, Paxten straightened.

The new troops drew rein, and behind them rumbled a black carriage drawn by a team of six steaming, dark bays. Harness rattled and the coachman slowed the team to a halt.

At this new arrival, the soldiers on the quay turned. Paxten watched, amazed. Of all things, their captain started shouting orders for them to stand at attention.

Alexandria edged closer to him. "What is it?"

He lifted one shoulder, then said, "I think it is more *who* is it—the commander at Dieppe, perhaps?" He took her hand and looked down at her. Then he flicked his thumb across the corner of her mouth. "Ah, *ma chère,* it has been a good fight. But it's done. You can't fight all of that."

He gestured to the troops now lining the quay, their horses hot from galloping, and tossing their heads, the soldiers' eyes forward and alert, and the faces under their plumed shakos rigid masks.

Alexandria's shoulders slumped. She glanced at her niece. "Dear, a poker will not do. Not any longer."

Nodding, Diana allowed the iron to clatter to the cobblestones. Then she came to her aunt's side, her hands shaking but her chin up and her face composed.

And then Paxten muttered, his voice low and rough, "Mother Mary, it is worse than I thought."

Alexandria looked up at him, but Paxten could only gesture to the black coach.

At first, she saw only a small man in a dark greatcoat. He stood beside the carriage, a black bicorne on his head and his glance sweeping around as if to take in everything in an instant. His plain clothes—dark coat, white waistcoat, breeches, and cravat, and low-cut black boots—seemed that of a merchant. He stood no taller than any man, but he had not the air of a merchant. Without effort, he dominated the scene.

Then he turned to stare at them, and Alexandria's heart skipped. She recognized that swarthy, heavy face with the burning dark eyes. She let out a breath. "The First Consul. It's Bonaparte!"

Sixteen

She had met him once, and only briefly, at Lord Whitworth's embassy ball. Now she hoped Bonaparte would remember nothing of that occasion, though he was noted for his quickness of mind. However, she looked far different now, in her gray satin, her hair tousled, and her bare feet dirty.

She glanced toward the captain, but she saw that despite his focus on the First Consul's arrival, he had not entirely forgotten Paxten. He had two men to face them, muskets at the ready. The rest he put at full attention, arms presented.

From the column of mounted officers, Bonaparte gestured to one man. The fellow wheeled his horse from the others and trotted forward. Bonaparte said something to him. The man nodded and then spun his mount again, spurring the horse to a gallop and then plunging to a halt before Taliaris.

Alexandria found it difficult to watch anyone but the First Consul. He exuded power and quick intelligence. Had he always done so? Or had his rapid rise from the ranks of the Republican Army given him such an aura. She could not admire the man, but she found him fascinating. What could he want here, of all places?

She leaned to Paxten. "Dare we attempt a departure?"

Paxten glanced at Taliaris, now conferring with the officer sent to him by Bonaparte, and then to the ships behind them. One vessel seemed to be raising its sails and making ready to draw anchor. He looked at the soldiers set to watch them, and shook his head.

Frustration welling, Alexandria glanced back to Bonaparte. He had turned to his carriage and now helped out a woman—a lovely woman who smiled at him and laughed at something he said. The woman carried a small white dog in her arms.

Alexandria's jaw slacked, and shock rippled through her. "Paxten, is that—is that not—?"

"Madame D'Aeth. Well, well, I wonder what battle the general has been sent off to fight and die in for the First Consul and for France?"

They turned and watched as Taliaris strode forward to meet the man who had fought his path to ruling France.

Taliaris gave a stiff salute to the First Consul. He towered above Bonaparte, but he had no illusions as to who held command. He also kept his stare away from the woman who hovered in the background behind Bonaparte. He had recognized her at once, and he was not certain how to act now.

Bright dark eyes fixed on Taliaris. "I came to inspect my ports—but what am I inspecting here?"

"General, sir, we—that is, I—"

He could not help it. He glanced at Madame D'Aeth and stuttered into silence. How did he explain avenging the general for the dishonor of his wife without implying that the First Consul now also dishonored the woman?

His cravat tightened and he drew in a ragged breath, his thoughts turning fast.

Yes, he could mention rape. And an Englishman. Then he straightened. "I am here under orders from General D'Aeth."

There—that was an honest answer.

His expression bored, Bonaparte looked away, studying instead the harbor and the cliffs above it. "You are no longer under his command. General D'Aeth is posted to Santo Domingo."

Glancing at Madame D'Aeth, Taliaris searched her pretty face for a glimmer of regret or sadness. If she had shown any, he would have spoken. Instead, she bent to the little dog she held in her arms and cooed something at it.

He clenched his teeth. He had been defending nothing.

Nothing! His mouth dried to ashes. This woman had used her husband, and now she used France. Why she had taken a dislike to Marsett no longer mattered. But he knew now that she had not even the decency to worry for her husband. Nor had she interest, it seemed, in her own honor.

He had, however, seen real valor and love in the last few moments. His duty lay clear. He saluted the First Consul. "Sir, your permission to finish matters here?"

Bonaparte turned, smiled at the woman, petted her dog, and then turned back. "Do so. And then I wish a tour of the harbor. I want to know how many men could we station on the bluffs—and how deep is this harbor. Well? Why do you still stand here?"

Clicking his heels, Taliaris snapped a salute. Then he turned and strode back to the quay.

Marsett, Lady Sandal, and Miss Edgcot watched him, tense and wary.

Taliaris strode past his men and stopped before them. "By order of the First Consul, I am no longer under orders from General D'Aeth." He stepped nearer to them and added in English now, "I recommend you take advantage of that before the First Consul takes an interest in you and gives me new orders."

Turning, he barked commands to dismiss his troops. They glanced at him and then fell out, looking at one another and then back at Marsett, puzzled and glowering. But they went.

Taliaris turned to the English again. "Why are you still here?"

Paxten took Alexandria's hand. "We are gone already." He started with her for the docks, but she dragged at him until he had to stop. "Come, *ma chère*. The tide will not wait. We cannot lose this chance!"

Alexandria turned to him. "But Diana?"

Looking back, he saw the girl still standing in front of the captain. And he cursed.

Taliaris frowned at the girl. "Well? Why do you not leave? Is this not what you want?"

Diana nodded. "I—well, I thought someone ought to thank you. So . . . well, thank you."

He stared at her.

"You English have no sense! Go—before I change my mind."

She smiled. "As if you would. You are a man of honor, I see. That is a rare thing. I hope you never allow the world to take that from you."

His frown deepened, but he said nothing.

She glanced toward the First Consul's carriage, then looked at the captain. Bitterness lay in his eyes. She wanted to ease that from him. And so she said, the words pouring out in a rush, "There are women of honor as well. Please do not forget that."

The hard look eased from his eyes. "I know. Now hurry! The tide turns for you."

Smiling at him, she started to walk away. And then she thought of her aunt and Mr. Marsett and of regrets for things not done. Stopping, she glanced back.

Without another thought, she ran to him and threw herself at him, letting him catch her, knowing he would. Wrapping her arms around him, she kissed him. Kissed him because she wanted to. Because she had felt cheated earlier of his lips. Because . . . oh, just because.

He tasted of salt from the air and something else that settled inside her.

And then he put her on her feet and pushed her away.

Her smile widened. "This war cannot last forever. And I live in Surrey. In Wellings. At Edgcot Place. And . . . well, I want you to know, a man of true honor is worth any wait."

He shook his head and started to speak, but she said first, "Yes, I know—go! *Adieu, mon cher.*"

She turned and ran then, but she thought she heard behind her a low, rough *adieu*.

Mr. Marsett scolded her with a flurry of French, and Aunt Ali grabbed her hand and would not let go. They ran for the dock, and then Paxten herded them into a rowboat, almost throwing them in.

Diana did not notice. She watched the quay and a tall figure in a uniform. And she wondered if some things were fated? Such as her aunt and Mr. Marsett. Or was it all a matter of luck?

She turned away from the shore to find a fishing boat bobbing on the gray waters of the Channel before them. Glaring at it, she muttered, "I thought we would have a proper ship!"

Alexandria laughed. She glanced at the disappointment on her niece's face, and her last worry faded. She had wondered for a moment if perhaps Diana had conceived a too-sudden and too-rash attachment to that rather handsome captain. But now she relaxed. Diana was young. She wanted adventure. This had to be just another part of it.

Paxten hailed the boat, and soon enough a rope ladder fell over the side of the single-masted vessel. They climbed up the ladder, the two boats swaying, falling and lifting with the swells of the ocean. Alexandria's stomach dipped at each lurch, but at last she stood on the deck, Paxten and Diana with her.

The captain of the boat—a fat fellow with dark eyes and black hair worn slicked back—eyed them and said something to Paxten. Alexandria did not understand his words, but she could not mistake his meaning. She glanced at Paxten, almost ready to cry now, and muttered, "Heavens—the jewels! We have no payment!"

Diana turned away and seemed to pull something from her bodice. With a smile and a curtsy, she handed a ruby necklace, bracelet, and earrings set in gold to the captain. The man held up the stones, squinted at them, then grinned broadly and flourished gestures of welcome and for them to make themselves comfortable.

Alexandria stared at her niece. Diana smiled, lifted her shoulders in a too-Gaelic shrug, then explained. "I thought it best to go back for them before we left the inn this morning."

With a grin, Paxten swept the girl into a hug. He lifted her off her feet, realized he should not have, for pain jabbed his side, but he spun her around anyway. "You, *ma fille,* can have whatever you wish to ask of me."

"You may stop calling me your girl. I shall not be a girl

forever. In fact, I think I very much have stopped being a girl on this trip, and I ought to merit more consideration. Should I not, Aunt Ali?"

"Yes, dear. Now, would you care to go and sit someplace and watch the waves or some such thing?"

Paxten saw the girl glance from her aunt to him, and then realize the hint. "Oh, yes. Yes, I shall see if one of the sailors will teach me to make knots."

She took herself off then.

Paxten took Alexandria's arm and led her to the bow of the boat. Waves broke in white crests below them. The wind, sharp and crisp from the sea, blew stinging droplets from the ocean against them. To the right, the sun edged a crescent of orange glow above the horizon.

Alexandria stood with one hand pressed to her stomach.

He took her hand. "Ah, no sickness allowed. Trust me—stay on the deck and you'll not have your stomach turning up on you."

She wrapped her arms around herself. "I shall freeze, however."

Standing behind her, he wrapped his arms over hers. "That is what I am for, *ma chère.*"

Leaning against him, she smiled. "Is it done? Really done? Are we safe?"

"We are, unless we shipwreck, or pirates attack, or we are boarded by an English frigate and taken for French spies."

She pulled away from him to glare at him. "Paxten! I was looking for reassurance."

With a grin, he pulled her back into his arms. "We are as safe as we ever are anywhere. Only, I fear, I am not at all safe. Not from you. Tell me, *ma chère,* why did you decide that now you cannot leave my side? What changed?"

Twisting, she looked at him. "Perhaps I changed—or perhaps you changed. Or perhaps it was because I had the freedom to make my choice." She cupped his face with her hand. "Or perhaps I finally found the courage to live up to the name you once gave me—to be your Lady Scandal."

He scowled at her. "I don't like any of these reasons."

She turned in his arms so that she faced him. "Do you like the reason that I love you?"

He smiled, and a tightness around his heart eased. "Say that again—I think the wind took away your words."

"I love you! And I shall say it however many times you wish. A hundred. A thou—"

His kiss interrupted her. With a sigh she relaxed into his arms. And then he pulled back and grinned at her. "Cannot a captain of a ship marry a man and a woman?"

"Can he? Are you certain?"

He shrugged. "No. But why do we not let him. We can always marry later in a church. Or better still, elope so your family and mine cannot scowl at us when we wed."

She smiled at him, her eyes as brilliant as the sunlight on the sea. "What a scandal that would be."

Smiling, he tightened his arms around her. "Ah, but, *ma chère,* I assure you, there will be no scandal attached to the too-respectable Mrs. Paxten Marsett."

Epilogue

"You do know what they called his mother—do you not—Lady Scandal!"

The lady in gray fanned her face. "No! Is that so?"

The matron with a purple turban and satin gown nodded. "Oh, yes. She married a second time—to some Frenchman."

The young man standing near them who had appeared to be reading from a book now lifted his stare. He had vague blue eyes and blond hair that darkened at the ends to a pale brown. He smiled at them. "Half French, actually."

The two matrons stiffened. The one in purple gave him a startled glance, then smiled and said, her tone stiff, "Lord Sandal—what a surprise to see you at Lady Anderson's musical evening. You are not much out these days, I understand."

"I came for the music. Not the gossip. But if you must talk, do get it right. My stepfather is Mr. Paxten Marsett, he is half French, and with the war ended, I expect he may well come back into the titles taken from his father in France. You might not want to get on the bad side of my mother if she becomes a countess, you know. She'll be more than Mrs. Marsett then."

The matrons stuttered apologies, but he bowed, and as he left, he heard the whisper: "Mark my words—he'll be a Lord Scandal, he will!"

He smiled, then went to find his mother. She had gone into the garden—with Paxten of course. He made a good deal of noise crunching across the gravel. Over the years, he had learned how to avoid embarrassing scenes. Not that Paxten ever seemed to be embarrassed about being caught making love to his wife. But Mother tended to color up, and Jules found it . . . well, just a touch distasteful, if he were to be honest. Not the affection between them. But such physical intimacy seemed to him to be a rather vulgar thing he would rather avoid.

They were discreetly sitting next to a fountain with a statue of Cupid in the center, merely holding hands, when he found them. "I came to say my good-nights."

His mother stretched one hand to him. She looked well, he thought. Still lovely. The silver in her hair no more than an added interesting lightness, and her face lined only by smiles. "What? So soon?"

"Yes. The music is excellent—so rare to hear a good alto soprano, but the tattle that goes around does wear."

She frowned. "It is not that again? I vow, Paxten, can you not do something?"

He shrugged and smiled. "Ah, but *ma chère,* it would not do for me to call out old dowagers for duels."

Jules kissed his mother's hand. "Don't worry on my account. It doesn't bother me really, so it should not you. It is just a bore. Good night, Pax."

With a wave, he continued down the garden path.

Alexandria watched her son leave, and then she turned to Paxten. "There must be something we can do."

Taking her hands, he pulled her to her feet and into his arms. Her figure had thickened over the years in ways a man could appreciate. His hands now smoothed over the flare of her hips. "What do you suggest? For it sounds as if you have a plan already."

She leaned back and smiled at him. "I do. What do you think of Paris?"

He frowned. "What—did you not have enough of it eleven years ago?"

"But that is ages ago. And Diana is longing to make the trip. And we could take Jules as well."

"And enjoy ourselves with them along?"

"Young people can find their own amusements."

He stared at her. "We are not young still then?"

"Well, then, *very* young people can find entertainment for themselves. And, thank you, but I would rather not be very young again." Her arms tightened around his neck. "I prefer to be where I am."

She kissed him slowly, her lips lingering over his, then pulled away at last with a sigh.

He rested his cheek against hers. "I suppose with Bonaparte sent away to Elba, he cannot again spoil things for you."

"We ought to be grateful to him, really. He did save our lives."

"He did, *ma chère.* And I should prefer to thank him from a distance. However, if you wish Paris, let us go to Paris."

She smiled at him. "And perhaps we shall have a little adventure?"

Paxten glanced around them. Then he looked at his wife. "*Ma chère,* the adventure I had in mind was of making love to you under the stars."

"Did you?"

"I did. Lady Anderson's garden, I understand, has a most secluded grotto, with water tumbling around that might hide your cries of passion."

"My cries?"

"And shadows made so convenient for seduction."

Alexandria fanned her face. "You are a wicked man."

"Ah, *ma chère,* you have found me out."

She leaned against him, happy, utterly content. "I found you out years ago. And I am so very glad that I did. Now, just where might we find this grotto?"

He chuckled. "Ah, I can see Paris will be quite the adventure, indeed."

AUTHOR'S NOTE

Napoleon Bonaparte's order to arrest "all the English, from the ages of eighteen to sixty, or holding any commission from his Britannic Majesty, who are at present in France . . ." appeared in the *Moniteur* in May 1803. It can be argued that neither the English nor the French were really serious about making a lasting peace when they signed the Treaty of Amiens. England failed to follow the terms by not evacuating Malta. France failed with its continual interference in the states of Italy and in Switzerland. And the treaty lacked any trade terms that might have made peace possible. Bonaparte's intentions are perhaps best shown in his letter to his minister, Talleyrand, concerning a note from the English ambassador: "If the note contains the word ultimatum, make him understand that word means war; if the note does not contain it, get him to put it in, on the grounds that we must know where we are."

England, however, beat Bonaparte to the act by making their declaration first.

By July 1803, Bonaparte had ridden to Calais, and then to Boulogne, and from there rode along the coast. He was looking for, in his own words, "a very favorable spot for my plans." Those plans were the invasion of England. I've taken the liberty to have Bonaparte first make his trip to Dieppe. Bonaparte was also known for his flirtations and amorous intrigues, and he was not above sending inconvenient husbands elsewhere.

By February 1804, Bonaparte wanted 130,000 troops in

Boulogne. He planned that "with a good wind we need the fleet for only twelve hours." He did not factor in the English fleet, or that Admiral Nelson would repeat his other naval success again at Trafalgar. That battle cost Nelson his life and ended any hope of a French invasion of England.

By then Bonaparte had gone from struggling soldier to General of the Republic to First Consul for life to crowning himself Emperor of France. He would also go on to other, larger mistakes—such as the invasion of Russia—and to eventual defeat. First by the allied armies in 1814, and then again in the brutal Battle of Waterloo in 1815.

But those are all other stories for other books.

If you would like a bookmark for *Lady Scandal* or for any of my other books, write to me at Shannon Donnelly, P.O. Box 3313, Burbank, CA 91508-3313, or read@shannon donnelly.com.

More Regency Romance From Zebra

Available Wherever Books Are Sold!

Visit our website at **www.kensingtonbooks.com**.